The Halloween Haunting

A Tess and Tilly Mystery

by

Kathi Daley

Tess and Tilly Cozy Mystery

Chapter 1

Sunday, September 15

"Oh, I don't know, Tess," Doctor Brady Baker said as we stood side by side, looking at the dilapidated old house that hadn't been lived in since before I was born. "I know I said that I liked your idea to sponsor a haunted house as a fundraiser for the animal shelter, but I wasn't necessarily thinking of using a real haunted house."

I glanced at the town's veterinarian, animal shelter owner, and all-around nice guy, who was frowning so hard he'd created a crater in the center of his forehead. "The house isn't really haunted," I assured him in a tone I hoped conveyed confidence. "At least I don't think it is." I amended, realizing that, in the end, it was probably best to be perfectly honest. "There was that one event a while back, but I'm sure the whole thing can be explained by using a rational and scientific explanation."

"What event?" Brandy asked, with a look of suspicion in his eye.

I remained silent, hoping he'd just drop it.

"You said there was that one event. What event?" he asked again.

I took Brady by the arm and walked him toward the rusty front gate which served as access the property. "It was no big deal. Really. You know how rumors get started." I rolled my eyes and huffed out a short breath that was meant to be a laugh of indifference, but sort of came out as a laugh of panic. "Everything is going to be fine, and this event is going to be spectacular, you have a Tess Thomas seal of assurance on that."

"What event, Tess?" Brady asked, digging his heels in at the gate.

I hemmed and hawed, but eventually answered. "Well, there was this one tiny incident a few years ago."

"Incident?"

I crossed my fingers behind my back to nullify the tiny white lie I was about to tell. "It really wasn't a big deal. Sure, it made the news, and there was a short investigation, but if you ask me, the whole thing was blown way out of proportion."

"What whole thing?"

"This guy from out of state bought the house and planned to open a bed and breakfast, but apparently, there was some sort of problem with the electrical. The lights kept flickering on and off, and the kitchen appliances went all wonky. The guy tried to fix the problem himself rather than calling in an electrician, but I guess he didn't know what he was doing because something happened and he was electrocuted. The estate was sold after the man who was electrocuted died, and the guy who currently owns the estate has assured me that the electrical has been dealt with, but not to worry, I plan to call in an actual electrician to fix any remaining electrical problems." I paused, smiled, and then continued. "It's a good deal, Brady. The new owner has plans to sell the place this summer after he has time to give the house a facelift, but I told him about the expansion we planned for the shelter, and he agreed to let us use the place for our fundraiser free of costs."

"Free of costs?"

I took Brady's hand and pulled him through the gate. "There are a few minor repairs that will need to be seen to, and I told him I would take care of those repairs, but I can get volunteers to help out with that. I have folks who will donate supplies and others who will donate labor if it means the shelter can be expanded to include a state of the art dog training facility and long term residential care for senior animals and difficult to place pets. White Eagle, Montana, is a town that cares about its citizens, even its four-legged citizens. I have no doubt if we sponsor this haunted house, folks will come. A lot of them. It really is a good plan."

Brady looked somewhat dazed as he stared at the house. It had been abandoned decades ago and needed more than just a few repairs to make it livable, but we didn't want to live in it. We only wanted to borrow it. I'd had a contractor look at it and had been assured that the house had good bones and was structurally sound. Yes, there were items we would need to address before we could use it to host a public event, but I hadn't been exaggerating or lying when I said I had volunteers to see to that. Of all the old houses in the area, this house, with its creepy and unusual exterior and large plot of land, was the perfect place to create our haunted house.

"So what do you think?" I asked.

"It does look as if it could really be haunted."

"It does if you believe in ghosts." I looked at Brady. "Do you believe in ghosts?"

"Not really."

"Me neither," I said even though I knew that there had been ghost sightings in the past and there were those odd noises that I'd heard when my boyfriend, Tony Marconi, and I drove out a few nights ago to get a feel for how the place would look under the moonlight. Still, even if the place was haunted, I figured we could deal with that. The reality was the crumbling exterior, interesting clock tower, dark and brooding widow's walk, and shuttered windows were absolutely perfect for what I had planned. "The large flat area to the left is going to be the graveyard," I explained, as I steadfastly pulled Brady along behind me.

"Graveyard?"

Geez, the guy really was stunned. Hadn't he ever seen a house that may or may not be haunted before?

I nodded and grinned, barely able to contain my enthusiasm. "It's an additional fundraiser. Tony is going to make a bunch of wooden headstones that people can buy and inscribe with a short epitaph. We'll place them in the cemetery, and everyone who comes out for the haunted house tour will be able to read them while they wait in line."

"Line?"

"Yes, line. If we use this house for our haunted house, I guarantee you that folks will come all the way from Billings to see it."

Brady frowned. "Billings? Doesn't Billings have their own haunted house event?"

"Well sure, but they just use an old warehouse. Their haunted house doesn't come with a legend the way ours will."

He lifted a brow. "Legend?"

Oops. I probably shouldn't have used the word legend. "You know how it is with small towns and their old houses. They all seem to have a legend." I hoped I pulled off the cheery *no need to worry* tone I was going for.

"And what might the legend of this house be?" Brady asked.

I looped my arm through his. "Oh, we don't need to talk about that right now. Let's go inside."

"What legend, Tess?"

I huffed out yet another breath. I'd expected that Brady would need to be persuaded that the house was perfect for our event, but this was turning out to be a lot more work than I'd anticipated. "I guess there may or may not have been an old cemetery on this plot of land before the house was built, and I suppose there may or may not be those who believe the souls whose resting places were disturbed currently haunt the place."

He frowned. "Why would anyone build a house on top of a cemetery?"

I giggled nervously. "Oh, you know how it is. The cemetery hadn't been used since the gold rush and land in this area is expensive. I guess what it comes down to is that everyone is looking for a bargain, and a plot of land that was used as a cemetery a century earlier, presented a bargain to the man who built the house all those years ago."

"So someone actually built a house on top of peoples' graves?"

"No, silly." I playfully swatted at Brady's shoulder. "The remains of those who'd been buried on the land were moved to another location. Now, back to our fundraiser. I think once you see the interior, you are going to love this place as much as I do." I leaned forward and really put my weight into dragging this tall man, who had to weigh double what I did, the rest of the way down the walk.

"Okay, wait." Brady froze at the threshold to the front door. "Are you actually telling me that you want to hold our shelter fundraiser in a house built on land that was previously used to house a cemetery?"

I nodded.

"Are you crazy?"

"Do you want a state of the art training facility?"

"Well, yes."

"And do you want to have a place to offer permanent housing for elderly and hard to place dogs and cats?"

"You know that I do."

"And if you were the sort who was willing to pay, say twenty bucks, to walk through a haunted house, would you be more likely to fork over the big bucks to walk through the cafeteria at the high school or a real house that folks already say is haunted?"

Both Brady's brows shot up. "You think people will pay twenty bucks to walk through a haunted house?"

"I think they will pay twenty bucks to walk through *this* haunted house." I took in a long breath, held it, and then exhaled. "Look. I'm not thrilled that the guy who built this house more than a century ago built his home on land that should have been preserved as hallowed ground. And I'm not happy that the remains of those buried on that same plot of land a century before were moved. But things were looked at differently back then and not using this house as a fundraiser isn't going to undo any of that. It makes no sense to pass on the opportunity to raise the money we need to expand our ability to help homeless pets in the area."

Brady took a step back. He looked up at the tall structure in front of him. "Are you sure it is safe? As you just pointed out, this house is over a century old, and I know it hasn't been lived in for decades."

"I promise you that it will be safe once Tony and his band of elves get done with the place. Mike has even arranged for the county inspector to give it the green light before we begin decorating for the event."

Mike Thomas was my brother and a local police officer.

"And you think people will actually come from as far away as Billings to see the place?"

"I think droves of people will come out to see the place once *Haunted America* airs."

Brady turned and looked at me. "*Haunted America*?"

"TV show. Super popular. I know a guy who knows a guy who made the arrangements."

Brady froze. When he did not speak or move for more than fifteen seconds, I was afraid I'd shorted out the poor guy's brain.

"Look," I continued in my most persuasive voice. "I know this is a little out of the box for a fundraiser, but it is October, and everyone is into the spooky vibe. The plans we discussed for the expansion to the shelter are huge, which means that even with the large donation Tony has already made, we still need a huge fundraiser to afford to do them. A kiddie carnival or pet parade is not going to cut it. We need to go big, and a real haunted house which will be featured on *Haunted America* just about the same time our haunted house opens is exactly the sort of fundraiser that is going to get us to where we need to be. So what do you think? Are you going to go big or are you going to be the guy who passed up the chance to do something amazing?"

Brady hesitated.

"Come on, Brady. Take a chance. For the animals. For the town."

"Okay. I'm really not sure about this, but I guess we're going to go big." Brady put his hand on the doorknob. He gave it a twist and pushed the door open. I was glad I'd come by and unlocked it earlier or our dramatic moment might have been ruined. He took a step into the entry and froze. His mouth dropped open as he looked around at the large space. "Are you sure it isn't going to cost more to make this place usable than we are going to make in ticket sales?"

"I'm sure. Do you want to see the second story?"

Seconds after I asked my question, there was a crash overhead.

"Uh, thanks, but I think I'm good." Brady took a step back toward the still open door. "You've never steered me wrong in the past, and I have no reason to think you would steer me wrong now, so I guess I'll get busy on a press release letting everyone know that the White Eagle Animal Shelter is going to throw one heck of a fundraiser this year."

Chapter 2

Monday, October 7

"Morning, Hap," I said to Hap Hollister, owner of the only hardware and home supply store in town.

"Morning, Tess. Tilly," he expanded his greeting to include my dog, Tilly, who, as she did every weekday, was out delivering the daily mail with me.

"I love what you've done with your window. The bales of hay, scarecrows, pumpkins, baskets of apples, and fall leaves provide passersby with both the feel of the harvest and the feel of autumn and Halloween."

"Exactly the mood I was going for. Did you notice the chainsaw sitting next to the log with the ax in the center of the window?"

"I did."

"I have chainsaws on sale this month, so the window was designed to both entertain and provide advertising."

I glanced back toward the window. "It really is perfect. If I needed a chainsaw, I'd buy one, but Tony took care of cutting, splitting, and stacking my wood for the winter. I might want one of those red scarves the lumberjack scarecrow is wearing if you have those for sale."

Hap reached behind the counter and took out a red knit scarf. He handed it to me. "It's a gift. I think red will look good on you with your dark hair."

I accepted the scarf. "Thanks, Hap. I love it. Are you sure I can't pay you for it?"

He shook his head. "I have a couple left from last Christmas and am happy to pass it along. By the way, did the supplies for the haunted house I sent over get to you okay?"

"They did, and thanks again." I set the stack of mail I'd brought for him on the counter. "You've donated so many supplies for the event that I'm going to add you as a sponsor. I just wasn't sure if you wanted to be listed by name or if you wanted the sponsorship to be listed as the hardware store."

"A shout out for the store would be great, but you know I was happy to make the donation, even without the recognition."

I smiled at the white-haired man. "I know, and that is what makes you such a special person." I took the lid off the candy dish Hap kept on his counter and popped a butterscotch into my mouth. I had a long route covering the entire downtown section of White Eagle, and I usually liked to keep moving, but there were certain businesses which required more than a drop and run, and Hap's store was one of them.

"Did you get that electrical glitch you've been having worked out?" Hap asked, after setting his outgoing mail on the counter.

"Not yet. The lights are still flickering even though we've had the electrician out twice. The folks from *Haunted America* will be here on Wednesday to film the segment they plan to air on the sixteenth, so Tony is going to see if he can figure it out before then. If not, I think that the *Haunted America* staff might be just as happy to have the lights flicker. It is, after all, a show about actual haunted places."

"I guess you might be right about that. I take it you are going to wait to decorate the house for the fundraiser until after the filming. I'm sure the *Haunted America* folks will want the house to look as authentic as possible."

I nodded. "They do want to film before we decorate, so I've scheduled the *Haunted America* folks on Wednesday of this week. They will spend the night in the house and will leave Thursday. The segment will air on Wednesday, October sixteenth. I have a whole passel of volunteers coming on Friday, October eleventh, to decorate for the haunted house. I figure with all the mechanical props Shaggy has tracked down, it will take the entire weekend to get everything set up. The haunted house runs two long weekends, Friday – Sunday, plus Halloween night. Opening day will be on October eighteenth. I went ahead and started the presale for the tickets early, and we've already sold out for both the Friday and Saturday of opening weekend. I think this venture might turn out even better than I'd planned."

Hap leaned his forearms on the counter in front of him. "You know I'm pulling for you and the animals. I think your idea of building permanent housing for hard to place pets is inspired. If you need anything at all once you start decorating, you just let me know."

"Thanks, Hap. I really appreciate it."

I chatted with Hap for a few more minutes, and then Tilly and I continued on our route. Fall in White Eagle was about as pretty as you would find anywhere. The trees were painted in shades of red, orange, and yellow, and the sky was sunny and blue in spite of the crisp hint of winter in the air which served as a reminder that the first snow was right around the corner.

"Morning, Aunt Ruthie," I said after entering Sister's Diner, the restaurant my mom, Lucy Thomas, and my aunt, Ruthie Turner, owned together. I always enjoyed spending extra time each day at the diner, but when the air outside was cool, and Ruthie greeted me with a cup of hot coffee and a freshly baked cinnamon roll, my delivery stop at the diner almost always turned into my morning break.

"It's chilly out today," Ruthie commented.

I nodded as I slipped my mailbag off my shoulder, tossed it into a nearby booth, instructed Tilly to crawl beneath, and then accepted the coffee and roll. "I heard it might snow by the end of the week. I'm sure it won't amount to much, but the cold turn does serve as a reminder that I should start putting away my deck furniture and getting my cabin winterized."

"I'd think that handsome boyfriend of yours would take care of chores like that," Ruthie said as she sat down across from me.

"He usually does, and I'm sure he will once I fill him in on the impending snow, but he's been putting in a lot of hours at the haunted house. I'm not even sure he realizes they are calling for snow by the end of the week."

"The cooler weather has sort of snuck up on us," Ruthie agreed. "And I'm sure Tony is busy. I've wondered how his work with the haunted house has affected his work with his friend, Shaggy, and the game they've been developing. I seem to remember they wanted to have it ready for testing before Christmas. Are they still on track for that?"

Tony was a computer genius, and Shaggy owned a video game store. They were both heavily into gaming, and according to Tony, the game they were working on was going to be revolutionary.

"The amount of time Tony has spent working on the house has set them back a bit, but we are heading into winter, and the slow season, so I'm sure they can make up the lost time. I'm not sure about the Christmas deadline, but knowing Tony, he'll do what he needs to do to meet his commitments." I took a bite of the cinnamon roll. "Did you do something different to the frosting? It's good. Different, but really good."

"Your mom has been trying out different flavors. Yesterday was caramel and the day before was almond. I think she added a hint of peppermint to the frosting today."

"I like it. And I think the variety is fun. I'm sorry I missed the caramel. That sounds delicious."

"It was very popular, so I'm sure she'll do that one again. I'll save you one when she does."

"Thanks. I appreciate that. Where is Mom anyway?"

"She is attending the committee meeting for Christmas on Main."

I raised a brow. "Are they going to do that again this year? I thought the committee decided it was too much work and they were going to try a different type of fundraiser."

"They were going to try something less labor-intensive this year, but then they found a woman who works as an event planner. Her name is Virginia Wellington, and apparently, she was willing to take on the project for a very reasonable fee. The committee discussed it and decided to hire her. I guess they are even planning to expand the event to include a carnival with rides and kiddie games. They plan to set it up in the field next to the park."

"What if it snows?" White Eagle was far enough north that a white Christmas was pretty much a given.

Ruthie shrugged. "Apparently, the committee doesn't care if it snows. In fact, your mom mentioned that a little snow drifting through the air while visitors ride on the Ferris Wheel would be romantic. And I suppose she has a point. As long as it is just a little bit of snow and not a blizzard, which as we both know, has happened from time to time even in December."

I wrapped my arms around my shoulders and faked a shiver. "Sounds cold to me, but I guess if the committee is on board, I'm on board. Christmas on Main is a fun event, and I was sort of bummed when I heard they weren't doing it this year." I glanced at the clock and pushed the remainder of my cinnamon roll to the center of the table. "I really should get back to my route. Do you mind wrapping this up for me? I'm sure I'll be hungry later."

"Sure thing. A snack for later will be just the thing. I hear you've been working yourself ragged trying to get your haunted house ready for the *Haunted America* crew."

"It's been a lot of work, but I really think it is going to be something special, and I think it is going to make a lot of money for the shelter which is, after all, the most important thing."

"It is. You and Brady are to be admired for the commitment you've shown for the homeless animals in the area. The fact that this community supports the shelter the way it does is a testament to the folks who live here as well."

I picked up my bag and flung it over my shoulder. "I couldn't agree more."

The next hour flew by as I dropped off mail, picked up outgoing letters, and knocked out a good portion of my route. I knew that I'd need to stop and chat when I arrived at the Book Boutique, the bookstore owned by my best friend and new sister-in-law, Bree Thomas. Bree had established long ago that unless the town was literally on fire, as my best friend, I owed her, at the very least, a good five to ten minutes of chitchat when delivering her mail.

"Your brother is a pig," she said the minute I walked in the door.

Uh oh. I turned around and looked down the street, half hoping for a fire. "What did he do now?"

Her face turned red. "You mean other than go out of his way to make my life a lot harder than it really needs to be?"

I groaned. It seemed that Mike and Bree had suffered a few growing pains now that the two of them were married and living together full time. "Yes, other than that. I know he has been getting on your nerves lately, but what has he done *this* time to make you so mad?"

Bree huffed out a breath and walked around the counter. She stood next to me, leaning a hip on the counter. "I had my book club last night. The Sunday book club at the church, not the Thursday book club I have here. Anyway, when I got home, I was greeted with what could only be described as having had a tornado blow through my kitchen. I swear every pot and pan I own was dirty. I tried to keep it together, and as calmly as I could, I asked why he hadn't cleaned up his mess if he'd decided to cook for himself, to which he responded that he'd get to it later. Later? Seriously? By this point, the food was so stuck on them that I seriously considered tossing them and buying new pots and pans."

I wasn't at all surprised that Bree and Mike were having this particular problem. Bree considered it a mortal sin to leave a single dish in the sink, and Mike was the sort to use a letter opener as a knife if all the knives were dirty.

"You knew Mike was a slob before you married him," I pointed out.

Bree groaned. "I did, but I just had no idea how much of a slob he really was. Before we were married, he at least pretended to try to pick up after himself, but now that there is a ring on my finger, he acts like he has a dish fairy following him around who will take care of things if he leaves the dishes sitting out long enough."

"So stop being his dish fairy, and he will stop counting on it."

Bree looked at me with doubt in her eyes. "Are you sure about that?"

Was I? "Actually, no," I answered honestly. "My mom waited on Mike hand and foot for his entire life. She even did his laundry and made his bed right up until he moved out. After he got his own place, his apartment looked like an 'A-bomb' had been set off inside pretty much the entire time he lived there. There is no doubt about it; Mike is a slob. I honestly think being a slob is hardwired into his circuit board. I really don't know if he'll ever change, but if you'd like me to talk to him, I will."

"No. That's okay. I married him; I guess it's up to me to fix him."

Fix him? Oh, sure that ought to go over well.

"Do you remember your wedding day?" I asked, after thinking things over for a moment.

"Of course, I remember." Bree's expression seemed to shift. Her scowl turned to a soft smile as she remembered the event. "It was perfect; the two of us standing under the stars professing our love for each other with our families looking on."

"And do you remember what you said to my slob of a brother while looking into his eyes and reciting the vows you had written?"

Bree groaned. "I said I loved Mike, and while we didn't always see eye to eye, I was willing to accept him into my life just as he was."

I raised a brow.

"I know what I said, but seriously, did he have to use every pot and pan in the house to make a single meal?"

"Apparently, he did." I glanced down at Tilly, who was waiting patiently by my side. "I need to make this a short visit today. I'm supposed to meet up with Tony at the haunted house as soon as I get off. We are hoping to finish up everything we need to for the inspection tomorrow."

"Do you feel like you're ready?"

I shrugged. "I hope so. We've been working hard, and I think we've tackled everything on the list except the problems we've been having with the electrical."

"Didn't some guy die messing with the electrical on that house?"

"Yeah, a long time ago. Tony knows what he is doing, so no need to worry."

"Maybe, but all the same, please be careful. I'd hate for Tony to end up as nothing more than crispy bits of burnt flesh. You do realize he is probably the perfect guy for you. He won't be easy to replace if he gets himself blown up."

I laughed. "Tony is not going to get blown up or electrocuted. He's much too smart for that. And I do know that Tony is the perfect guy for me and that he'd be impossible to replace. I really do need to run, but think about what we discussed before you talk to Mike again. The wrong approach will just make him dig his heels in, and then you'll never get him to wash a dish."

"I know. And thanks for the advice."

Chapter 3

By the time Tilly and I arrived at the house, Tony and his dog, Titan, were already there. A few other volunteers lingered in the area, but the house was mostly ready for the inspection tomorrow by the county. An inspection and a permit were necessary for us to get insurance for a commercial endeavor, so I was putting a lot of weight on making sure everything that needed to be done would be done in time. As I'd mentioned to Hap, the only real problem we were still faced with was the flickering lights.

"I know we've traced the wires back to the main electrical panel, so it seems like the interference must be occurring somewhere between the electrical outlet and the source," Tony said after I'd kissed him hello.

"I don't really understand what you mean. Where would there be something to interrupt the flow of the electricity other than in the lines?"

Tony squinted, biting his lower lip as he considered things. "I'm not sure. It really is odd the lights don't flicker all the time. It is almost as if the interference comes and goes. Take the light on the second-floor landing. That light has been flickering since day one, but only at times. Other times, it is perfectly fine. And if you trip the breaker in the main box in the attic, the light on the second-floor landing goes out completely, along with all the outlets in the hallway. It makes sense that the wiring for the entire landing and hallway runs up through the ceiling and then up the interior wall of the second bedroom and into the attic where the breaker box is located. I just have to wonder if it makes a direct trip or if the wiring takes a detour at some point between the outlet and the breaker."

I frowned as I watched Tony, who stood on a ladder with a flashlight, sorting through wires of varying colors. "I'm not sure what you are getting at. Why would anyone run wiring from one location to another and not take a direct route?"

"I don't know," he answered. "Most people wouldn't. Unless the wire splits somewhere to provide additional outlets that were added to the house after it was constructed. I'm going to go up into the attic and take another look around. I'm pretty sure the only way to know for sure what is causing the interruption is to open up the walls and actually eyeball the wiring, which I don't plan to do at this point since we have an inspection tomorrow, but maybe if I can make a small hole in the wall about halfway between this point and the breaker box, I can get a better feel for what might be going on."

Tony was a genius, and I trusted his instincts. Sure, his area of expertize was computers and not electrical contracting, but Tony had done a lot of upgrades to the electrical system in his home to handle the special needs of his very high-end equipment, so I figured if there was a possibility that someone had spliced into the wire that provided electricity to the hallway, he'd be able to figure it out. Still, I couldn't help but be reminded of Bree's warning about the man who'd already died while trying to fix the wiring in the old house and reminded Tony to be careful. He assured me he would as I followed him into the attic and then stood next to him while he stood in the middle of the room, staring at the wall. I figured he was going through the options in his mind, so I waited quietly, as did Tilly and Titan, who were sitting at my feet. Eventually, he walked up to a wall and began knocking on it. After several minutes of him doing this, I finally asked him what he was doing.

"This wall looks wrong."

I narrowed my gaze. "What do you mean, wrong?"

"It feels like it is in the wrong place."

I stared at the wall, but couldn't see what he was talking about.

"If this wall is an exterior wall, the ceiling is all wrong," Tony continued. "Since the attic is the only space on the top floor, all the walls should be exterior walls, yet this one is off."

Okay. I understood what Tony was saying. I think. I wasn't as spatially adept as he was, so I still couldn't actually see what he was talking about, but I understood. "So you think the wall is a fake wall and not an exterior wall?"

"Exactly."

"Maybe whoever built the attic didn't want such a large space to finish off, so they used interior walls to minimize the space."

"Maybe."

I jumped when Tony picked up a hammer and punched a hole in the wall.

"Geez, you could have warned me," I said, placing a hand on my chest. "You nearly scared me to death."

"Sorry." He pulled the sheetrock away. The space behind the wall was dark, and the air was musty, but it was definitely another interior space and not the exterior of the house. I guess Tony's hunch had been right after all.

"Can you see what's back there?"

Tony shook his head. "It's too dark. Hand me that flashlight."

I looked around the room and then picked up the flashlight from the pile of tools Tony had left on the floor from his work on the electrical panel. I crossed the room and handed it to him. He shone it into the room on the other side of the wall, sticking his head in through the small opening he'd created.

"Well, I'll be damned," he said with a tone of amazement in his voice.

"What is it?" I asked while trying to look over his shoulder.

He stepped aside, and I stuck my head into the hole he'd created to find myself face to face with a skeleton.

Chapter 4

The next several hours were crazy. I called my brother, Mike, who showed up with the coroner. The skeleton was removed from the room behind the wall and taken to the morgue. During the excavation of the body, Mike found something even more surprising than the skeleton Tony and I had found. Inside the secret room was a ladder that led to the clock tower, and laying on the decking of the clock tower behind the old clock that hadn't worked in decades, was a second body. A fresher body; a body that couldn't have been placed there more than a week ago.

"Do you know who this is?" I asked Mike as he called the coroner back after he'd left with the first remains.

"I suspect that it is Joe Brown. His wife reported him missing a week ago."

"Joe Brown. That name sounds familiar," I said.

"He was one of your volunteers. He works as a contractor and came with Grange to help out with the various repairs."

Grange Plimpton was a local contractor who'd been volunteering at the shelter for years.

"So what is Joe doing up here in the clock tower?" I looked around the small room behind the face of the clock. "How did he even get up here? The only access I see is the ladder which it appears can only be accessed via the secret room, and when we broke through the wall of the secret room, it looked as if it hadn't been accessed in ages."

Mike pursed his lips. He drew his brows together and looked around. "I don't know how he got here, and I don't know why he is here. I suspect he was murdered and then his body was stashed here, but at this point, I don't even know that for certain." Mike rolled the man's head to the side with his gloved hand. "It looks like there was trauma to the head, but with all the decay, it's hard to know if a blow to the head was the cause of death. I guess all we can do at this point is let the medical examiner take a look and then take it from there."

"Did this man's wife report that her husband had disappeared from this house?" I asked.

"No. According to Nora Brown, her husband had been here at the house helping Grange with the needed repairs but had come home after they'd finished for the day. They'd had dinner and watched a little television. She'd had a headache and went to bed early. When she woke up the following morning, it was obvious that Joe had never come to bed, so she looked around the house, but both he and his truck were gone. She assumed he'd already gone to work, so she didn't worry since he often went in early. When he didn't come home that evening, she called one of the men Joe works with who told her that her husband had never come in that day. The wife waited until the following day thinking he might show up with a reasonable explanation, but when he didn't, she came down to the station and filed a missing person's report."

"And in a week, had you come to any conclusions as to what might have happened to the guy?" I wondered.

"To be honest, my money was on a mid-life crisis." Mike looked toward the sheet-covered body. "I can see I was wrong."

Tony walked up behind me. "The coroner is here. There isn't room up here for everyone, so maybe we should head downstairs and let them do what they need to do."

"Yeah, okay." I glanced at Mike. "Tony and I will be downstairs."

Once Tony and I left and made some room, the coroner headed upstairs with a body bag. Based on the look on his face, I was willing to bet that even he was befuddled by the way things were unfolding.

"Do you remember this guy?" I asked Tony after we'd decided to wait in his truck with the dogs rather than standing around in the main living area of the old house where we'd indicated we'd be. "Mike said he was a volunteer who was here with Grange."

Tony shook his head slowly. "I don't specifically remember him, but I do remember Grange showing up with a crew of five or six guys a week or so ago. They fixed the railing on the stairs, a few holes that someone had punched into the walls, the leaky roof, and a few other items. They were just here for one day, so I didn't really get the chance to speak to all of them."

I leaned my head back against the seat and looked at the house through the windshield. It was dark, but the lights in and around the house were on so it wasn't too hard to see Mike and the others moving around inside. "So this guy shows up with Grange, spends the day doing simple repairs, goes home and has dinner with his wife, and then returns after she goes to bed? Why?" I asked. "And who killed him? Did he meet someone here? And if he did, who did he meet and why did he meet them?"

"And if he hadn't accessed the secret room and the ladder leading from the secret room to the clock tower, how did he end up in the tower in the first place?" Tony added.

"When we found the skeleton in the secret room, I really thought that would be the oddest thing to happen to us during this event, but I guess the skeleton was only the beginning."

"So, what now?" Tony asked.

I turned my head slightly. "What do you mean?"

"Are you going to cancel the inspection tomorrow? The TV show? The fundraiser?"

I slowly shook my head. "No, not unless Mike makes us cancel for some reason. I'm intrigued by the skeleton, and I think the folks from *Haunted America* will be too. I'm sorry about the contractor, but a lot of people have donated time and supplies to make this happen, and I really think this is one of those cases where the show must go on."

Tony turned and looked through the windshield toward the house. "I wonder if there are any other secret rooms or hidden spaces."

"Maybe," I answered. "The existence of one secret room does open the possibility in my mind."

"The house is very unique. The fact that the man who built it would include a widow's walk or a clock tower is surprising since these aren't the sort of items you normally find built into houses in this area, but to find both in one house, makes me wonder if there are other surprises that are just waiting to be uncovered."

I turned and looked out my side window at the large plot of land that came with the house. The place really was isolated, which is one of the things that attracted me to it in the first place. "Do you think we should look for other secret rooms or passages?"

"Maybe, but not until after the inspection. We're going to have a hard enough time getting the permit we need once the inspector finds out we've uncovered not one, but two bodies."

"Do you think he'll turn us down?"

Tony shrugged. "I don't know. I hope not. I suppose he might want to wait to issue the permit until after the police have processed the place. The haunted house is a week and a half away, but the *Haunted America* filming is in just two days, so even if he feels the need to wait on the permit for the event that will be open to the public, maybe he'll go ahead and allow us to film the television show."

"I don't think we need a permit for that. The television crew isn't paying us to use the house, and the filming isn't open to the public."

Tony opened his door. "Here comes Mike. Let's see what he has to say."

Chapter 5

Wednesday, October 16

It had been over a week since Tony and I had found the skeleton in the secret room and the body of Joe Brown in the clock tower, but other than the fact that the house had been processed and released for use, very little progress had been made in either case. The skeleton was still unidentified, and Mike had no idea why Joe Brown had gone back to the house on the night he disappeared, or how he'd ended up dead. Mike did know that the cause of death was blunt force trauma to the head and that the time of death was some point in the overnight hours after his wife had left him watching television.

As I'd suspected, the gang from *Haunted America* had been thrilled with the discovery of both the skeleton in the secret room and the contractor in the clock tower. The way they'd told it, the deaths were spook related. I sincerely doubted our killer was a ghost, but hey if the rumor that a ghost actually did live in the house sold more tickets to the fundraiser, which we had ended up receiving a permit for, who was I to deny it? I was curious to see what the publics' response would be when the segment aired this evening. The haunted event was due to open on Friday, and we'd already sold a lot of tickets, but not as many as I'd hoped. Still, once word got out that our haunted house was a real haunted house, I suspected the demand for tickets would exceed the supply.

"It's going to start in a few minutes," Bree said after settling in on the sofa next to Mike. It looked like the couple had made up, which I was happy to see. In spite of their differences, they really did seem perfect for each other, and I was pulling for their marriage to go the distance.

"I'll grab Tony," I said. We were at his house to watch *Haunted America*, and he'd wandered off at some point to take a call and had never come back.

"Okay, but hurry," Bree said. "You don't want to miss the beginning."

I headed toward the kitchen, which was the direction I'd last seen him heading. He was still on the phone, so I waved at him and then pointed toward my arm as if pointing toward a watch, which I was not wearing. He nodded, and I heard him tell whomever he was talking to that he needed to go but would call them back the following day.

"Who was that?" I asked as we headed toward the living room where Mike and Bree were waiting.

"Nona. I'd called and left a message that our trip was going to need to be postponed until after the first of the year and she was just returning my call."

Hello to the guilt. Tony had been asking me to go to Italy with him so that he could introduce me to his grandmother for months, but I'd been stalling. I loved Tony, and I wanted to meet the one person in the world who seemed to mean the most to him, but I was scared. I knew that Tony put a lot of stock in Nona's opinion. In fact, he had told me as much on more than one occasion. This made things tricky for me. I mean, what if she hated me? What if all she saw when we met was some skinny white girl who'd never even gone to college? Would her opinion influence how Tony felt about me? Would he break up with me if his grandmother didn't approve of our relationship? I was way too scared to find the answers to these questions, so every time Tony brought up the subject of the two of us taking a trip to Italy, I came up with an excuse to put it off.

Of course, I knew I wouldn't be able to put it off forever. At some point, I'd need to bite the bullet and meet the woman, or at least tell Tony why I was hesitant to do so in the first place. Going all the way to Italy seemed intimidating in and of itself. Maybe she could come here for a visit where I could meet her on my turf.

Bree hurried us up once we arrived in the main living area. The music had played, and the intro segment was just about to begin.

"Welcome to *Haunted America* where paranormal experts delve into the most haunted places you are likely to find in this great country of ours," the announcer said. "Tonight paranormal experts, Robert

Cobalter and Evan Turner, will explore the unusual happenings at a century-old mansion in White Eagle, Montana."

The man went on to provide a history of the house, including the fact that it had been built on a cemetery. He sort of made it sound as if they'd built the structure right over the top of the bodies that had been buried there during the nineteenth century, but I supposed that the idea that the bodies were still beneath the foundation of the home provided a spookier feel than an explanation that the bodies had been relocated to another cemetery before the structure was built.

By the time he got to the part about the skeleton in the secret room and the body in the clock tower, even I was sitting on the edge of my seat.

As planned, Robert and Evan had spent the night in the house. During the overnight hours, they'd recorded every creak and groan, every flickering light, and every shadow, whether real or imagined. They actually had me believing that the house was haunted even though, as Tony had assured me, there was most likely a reasonable explanation for every phenomenon we'd witnessed, including the lights that seemed to flicker for no apparent reason.

"Okay, so how did they manage to record that shadow that crossed the wall?" Bree asked as the announcer indicated that there would be a break for a commercial announcement. "It really did look as if they'd captured the movement of a being from another dimension."

"I'm sure the folks from *Haunted America* enhance the footage they record to make things look a bit more real," Mike said.

"Do you think they used computer imagery to create the effect?" I asked.

Mike shrugged. "Maybe, or maybe their lighting guy is just really good and can create the sensation of movement by recording everyday objects from different angles. I'm really not sure how they do it, but I am sure that you don't actually have a ghost."

"Maybe not, but we do have a skeleton and a murder victim," I pointed out, just as the first commercial of the set came on. "Any news on either one?"

"The skeleton, no. It's been entombed in that room for a long time. In fact, it looks like it might have been placed in the room before the last resident who lived in the house moved in."

Bree made a face. "Someone lived in a house where there was a skeleton just upstairs and they never even knew it?"

"It looks that way. The last family to actually live in the house was the Jordan family, who lived there from nineteen sixty-two until nineteen eighty-five. After the children left home, Mr. and Mrs. Jordan decided to move into a smaller place in Missoula. They put the house up for sale, but interest rates were crazy back then, so the place never sold. After Mr. Jordan died and Mrs. Jordan moved to the east coast, the oldest son, Alan, put the house up for sale again. He sold it to Jim Smith, who was electrocuted while trying to fix the flickering lights. For one reason or another, no one has lived in the house since the Jordans moved out in nineteen eighty-five."

"And the skeleton in the secret room?"

"The coroner seems to think the body in the secret room could have been put there as early as the nineteen-thirties or forties, but he doesn't know for certain. I suppose it is equally as likely that it was placed there much more recently, but the coroner seems to think the body has been in the room for more than fifty years."

"Assuming the coroner is correct, and the body has been entombed in the room since the thirties or forties, who owned the house then?" Tony asked.

"A woman named Ethel Vandenberg owned the house before the Jordans. She inherited the house from her father, Edward Vandenberg. Ethel was an only child who'd been raised by her overbearing and cruel father after her mother died when she was seven. She never married nor had children of her own. She lived in the house from the time she was born in nineteen eleven until she died under mysterious circumstances in nineteen sixty. The house stood empty until the Jordans moved into it in nineteen sixty-two."

"So was it Ethel's father who moved the cemetery and built the house in the first place?" I wondered.

"It was. He actually built the house for his first wife, Elizabeth, in eighteen ninety-seven. She fell from the widow's walk and died in nineteen hundred and five."

"I didn't realize there was access to the widow's walk," I said. "It looks as if it is strictly ornamental."

Mike answered. "I've not found access to the structure, and it does seem as if it was added as a decorative feature, but if Elizabeth did actually fall from the dang thing, there must have been access to it at one point in time."

"So what happened after Elizabeth died?" I asked.

"From what I can tell, Edward remained single until he married Ethel's mother, Barbara, in nineteen hundred and nine. Ethel was born in nineteen eleven, and Barbara died in nineteen eighteen due to a fall down the stairs which resulted in her breaking her neck."

"Two wives who both fall to their death. Seems suspicious," I said.

Mike nodded. "I agree. If Edward was still alive and the deaths were more recent, I'd definitely dig into things a bit."

"So if the skeleton we found was walled into the secret room in the nineteen-thirties or forties as the coroner suspects, then Ethel's father, Edward, must have put it there," Bree said. "I suppose Ethel might have, but it seems as if the father is a more likely suspect."

"It is my impression at this point that it was Edward Vandenberg who is responsible for the body being in the secret room," Mike confirmed.

"So the guy was probably a psycho killer who killed both his wives, plus this unknown woman," Bree added.

"The skeleton belonged to a male," Mike corrected.

"The show is back on," I said hushing everyone. As interesting as this conversation was, and it was interesting, I didn't want to miss anything the folks from *Haunted America* had to say. I had to admit that the hosts who narrated the segment really did a good job of leaving the choice to believe in ghosts or not up to the viewer. They didn't try to convince you that the house was haunted as a lot of similar shows did.

They just presented the facts, or at least the facts according to them, and then let the viewer decide.

After the show ended, Tony offered everyone dessert. I'm not sure how I'd ended up with a boyfriend who was not only a genius with a computer but was also a genius in the kitchen, but I considered myself lucky that I had. I would most likely have gained a ton of weight since Tony and I started dating if not for the fact that my job required me to walk miles and miles every week.

"So what's going on with the contractor in the clock tower?" I asked Mike as we enjoyed our apple cobbler with vanilla ice cream and hot cinnamon topping.

"I still can't explain how he got to be there since it doesn't appear he, or anyone, had accessed the secret room at the time he was left in the clock tower. The only explanation I can come up with is that Joe met someone at the house and both he and the person he met accessed the clock tower using a ladder to get onto the first story of the roof and then climbed up from there."

"Seems like a risky venture."

"It does, but I can't really think of another explanation. I figure that once Joe and the individual he met were in the tower, the person with Joe hit him over the head with a blunt object which resulted in Joe's death. The killer then climbed down the ladder, taking it with them when they left since a ladder was not found at the house or in Joe's truck."

"So you found Joe's truck?" I asked.

Mike nodded. "I tracked it down to a wooded area not far from the Vandenberg house. I'm not sure if Joe parked it there when he returned to the house to prevent it from being seen from the road, or if the killer moved it after he'd left Joe's body in the clock tower."

"Your theory sounds like it might have merit," I agreed. "Although it is a tall house, so the ladder used would need to be pretty tall as well, even to get to the first story."

"Joe did work as a contractor," Mike reminded me. "I'm sure he had access to all sorts of ladders. The questions in my mind are: who did Joe meet, and why did he go back to the house in the first place?"

"Maybe Joe found something while he was at the house working on the repairs," Bree suggested. "Maybe something of value, such as a piece of jewelry a previous owner might have left behind. His plan might have been to access the house through an upstairs window. Maybe a window he intentionally left unlatched. He might have needed help, so he called a friend, but once they got here, the friend turned on him."

"Seems like as good an explanation as any," Mike agreed, which made Bree smile proudly.

"Actually, it's not a good explanation," I countered. "Why would Joe need help retrieving a piece of jewelry? In fact, why wouldn't he just put it in his pocket at the time he found it?"

"Maybe it wasn't jewelry," Bree defended. "Maybe he found a hidden safe, and he went back to try to get into it."

"That makes more sense," I agreed. "But Tony and I have been over every inch of that house and haven't come across a hidden safe."

Bree blew out a breath. "Okay, so maybe it was something else. The point is that maybe Joe went back to the house to retrieve something he found earlier in the day and he asked someone to meet him because he knew he would need help retrieving whatever it was he was trying to retrieve."

"Okay, say that's right, and Joe asked someone to meet him at the house. How are we going to figure out who Joe met?" I asked. "Given the fact that he seemed to have returned to the house late at night, there are most likely not going to be any witnesses."

Mike took a sip of his coffee and then answered. "I'm not sure how I'm going to figure this out. If someone he asked to meet him at the house killed Joe, then motive, or at least the normal motives I would look at in a murder case, don't seem to come into play. If Joe had been left for dead in a ditch, or in the alley behind his house, I'd looked for people with a grudge against the guy, but it seems unlikely that Joe asked someone he was having a problem with to meet him at an empty house in a deserted location in the middle of the night."

I supposed Mike had a point.

"What about Joe's phone records?" Tony asked. "He must have called whomever he met and arranged to meet them."

"I pulled the records for his home, business, and cell phones, and didn't find anything suspicious. The last person he called from his cell was his wife and based on the timing, I suspect he called her to let her know he was on his way home or maybe that he'd be late or perhaps that he needed to stop to pick something up, or something like that. I have a call into her so I can ask her why he called her that afternoon, but she is staying with her sister and not taking calls."

"And his home and business lines?" Tony asked.

"All the calls to his business lines were incoming. I imagine he never had a chance to return them. I listened to his messages, but they all seemed to relate to the jobs he had going on. Most of the calls to his home line appeared to be for his wife."

"He might have had a burner phone," I suggested.

"He may have," Mike agreed, "but if he did, that leaves me wondering why."

"Did you find evidence of a burner in his possessions?" Bree asked.

"No," Mike answered. "He didn't have a phone of any sort on his person when he was left in the tower. His cell was in the glove box of his truck. I briefly looked around his home right after his body was found, but his wife became agitated and asked me to leave after only a few minutes. I didn't have a warrant, so I left."

I frowned. "I would think she'd want you to find her husband's killer even if you snooping around was causing her stress," I said.

"Unless the wife is in on whatever it is that happened to her husband," Tony pointed out.

"Maybe he left a mess in the kitchen, and she decided to end her torment once and for all," Bree smiled innocently at Mike.

I placed a hand over my mouth to hide my grin. I really did want to stay neutral when it came to marital spats between my brother and my best friend, but Mike was a slob, and in the end, I knew Bree would win, so I guess I found myself supporting her in my heart.

"Do you have any suspects at all?" I asked.

"If you take the fact that Joe's body was found in the clock tower of a deserted house into account, I have no one. If you take the location where the body was found out of the equation, I have a few suspects in mind, although, in the end, not one of them could have actually killed Joe and then left him in the tower."

I leaned forward, resting my forearms on the table. "Okay. So let's go over the list anyway. Maybe something will make sense."

Mike took a sip of his coffee before he began. "If you remember, Joe came to the house to help out in the first place because Grange recruited him. Initially, I thought Joe worked for Grange, and, as it turns out, he used to, but about six months ago, Joe decided to leave Plimpton Construction and start his own business. I spoke to Grange, and he seemed fine with the fact that his best employee had quit and become his biggest competitor, but apparently, Grange's brother, Greg, who is also his business partner, has been having a lot of heartburn over the situation."

"So you think Greg might have killed Joe to get rid of the competition?" I asked.

"Not necessarily," Mike answered, "but he does seem to have a motive. According to others I know in town who also work in the construction trade, Greg considered Joe to be a backstabbing traitor who used the training he and Grange provided over the years to betray them."

"It does sound like he makes a good suspect," I said.

Mike nodded. "He does, although there is no way Joe would have called Greg and asked him to meet him that night. The two men weren't even speaking to each other."

"Okay, who else do you have?" I asked.

"Ford Newland. I guess Ford hired Joe to do some work for him and from what I understand, Ford was not at all happy with the quality of the work he received. He refused to pay Joe for the work which Joe insisted was perfectly acceptable, so Joe sued him. I did some digging, and it seems that arbitration was not working and the case was probably going to go to trial. That would have been a huge expense for both parties, but neither party wanted to back down."

"Sounds like a good motive to kill a person," I said.

"I agree that Ford would be a good suspect, but Ford is seventy-two years old. I really don't think he climbed up on the roof of the Vandenberg house and killed Joe. Besides, I really have no reason to believe that Ford even knew he was there. I guess the reality is the only person who would have known he was there in the first place is someone Joe told to meet him, and neither Greg nor Ford fit that bill."

Mike did have a point. Those people who had a beef with Joe would most likely not have even known he was at the house that night. "Any other suspects come to mind?"

"Just one, but like the others, while he has a motive, he really doesn't seem to have had the opportunity or the means. It seems Joe was in an auto accident two years ago. The accident was his fault, but he was never arrested even though the man driving the other car was paralyzed from the waist down as a result of the collision."

"So why didn't you arrest him if the accident was his fault?" Bree asked.

"The accident didn't occur here. It occurred in Missoula, so it was not up to me to arrest or not arrest him. Calvin Letterman certainly has a motive to want to do harm to Joe, but again, the person who killed Joe had to have been on the roof of the old house with Joe and Calvin is in a wheelchair."

"Yeah," I agreed. "As you've pointed out, it does seem that if Joe called someone and asked them to meet him at the house, then the person who killed him is more likely than not someone he considered to be a friend." In my mind, the fact that Joe was most likely killed by a friend seemed to make the whole thing a lot worse than it would have been if he'd been killed by an enemy.

Chapter 6

Friday, October 18

I woke in the middle of the night to hear thunder rumbling in the distance. "Please don't rain," I whispered into the dark, praying the storm would dissipate, change direction, or simply blow through. The last thing I wanted to deal with on opening night was a downpour.

Tony was sleeping on the far side of the bed, while my cats, Tang and Tinder, snuggled up between us. Tilly slept on the floor on my side of the bed, while Titan slept on the floor on Tony's side. If Tony and I married one day and decided to have children, I really had no idea where we'd fit them in if, as children do, they woke up in the middle of the night after suffering a nightmare.

I closed my eyes and tried to go back to sleep, but my mind was running a million miles a minute and refused to slow down in spite of my best effort to manifest *nothingness* in my mind. I'd convinced a lot of people to go along with my plans for the fundraiser, which made me feel like fail or succeed, it was all on me.

Tony assured me that we were ready. He'd gone through every detail and operated every prop the previous day. We'd done a dress rehearsal with the volunteers who'd agreed to dress as monsters, ghosts, ghouls, and goblins. I knew in my heart that we really were ready, but for some reason, my mind refused to let go of the pointless exercise of imagining every single thing that could even remotely go wrong and then magnifying the chaos that would be created tenfold.

After an hour of tossing and turning, I decided to get up. Tilly followed me, but the other animals stayed with Tony. We'd been at the haunted house late last night, so we'd stayed at my cabin which is a lot closer to town than Tony's house on the mountain is. I liked to think we divided our time between his place and mine fairly equally, but the reality was that we spent a good eighty percent of the time at his place and only twenty percent of the time at mine.

Of course, his place was larger and a lot nicer. My tiny cabin was fine for Tilly and me, but now that our family had grown, things had gotten a bit tighter. Still, I loved my cabin. It was my home. I really couldn't imagine giving it up to move in with Tony full time.

After making a cup of tea, I tossed a log on the fire and curled up on the sofa. Tilly jumped up and snuggled in next to me. I tossed a throw over the both of us and willed the warmth and comfort of the moment to penetrate the stress I'd been feeling. As I'd predicted, the ticket sales for the event had been phenomenal once the episode of *Haunted America* had aired. We were pretty much sold out if we were going to stick to the occupancy limits we'd set up in advance. The haunted house was set up to be experienced by each guest as part of a tour. Each tour lasted twenty minutes, which allowed us to do three tours per hour. We'd decided that we wanted to limit the tours to twenty people per tour, which meant that sixty people could be served every hour. Since we were open for four hours per night, that allowed us to sell two hundred and forty tickets per night, which at twenty bucks a pop, was forty-eight hundred dollars per night times seven nights. That seemed to me to be more than enough money to get started on the expansion Brady and I had dreamed up one night after a training session. Still, I had to admit that the urge to increase the limits we'd set up was strong. Would the experience really be any less awesome with say twenty-five people per tour rather than twenty? I knew that if we had more spots to sell, we could sell them. Maybe I'd see if I could get volunteers for Monday through Wednesday of Halloween week. I supposed we should get through this first night and see how things went before making any changes.

I ran my fingers through Tilly's long hair as I stared into the fire. The scent of the pumpkin candle I'd lit last night lingered even though I'd extinguished it before going to bed. I pulled the comforter closer to my chest as the wind which normally preceded an incoming storm howled outside my window.

The idea for expansion of the shelter had started out as a discourse between Brady and me regarding the training program we put each dog through and the advanced training we could expand upon with the right facility. With an expanded facility, we'd have room to recruit and train additional volunteers to handle the specialized training we offered for some of our potential adoptive parents. The better suited a dog and his human were, the more likely they were to be happy with each other for the long term.

Once we'd discussed the advanced training we would be able to offer, we'd begun to create a dream list which included a permanent home for hard to place dogs and cats. Brady and I tried really hard to make sure every dog and cat had a friendly and loving forever home, but there were some animals, such as those with medical issues or those who couldn't be broken of negative behavior patterns, who were destined to live out their lives at the shelter. Brady and I paid extra attention to those animals and made them as comfortable as possible, but a real house for them to live in with sofas to lounge on and a yard to play in right there on Brady's property seemed ideal to both of us.

"Of course," I said to Tilly, "a facility like that will take a lot more than we will make from this event, but Tony made a huge donation, so I'm hoping we'll make enough to add to his donation to get started."

Tilly thumped her tail on the sofa next to me.

"I wonder if Tony remembered to set out the tombstones."

Tilly raised her head and looked behind her.

"He remembered, but decided to wait and do it while you are at work today," Tony said, yawning as he entered the room looking all adorable and tousled. "I know we discussed putting them out last night, but I wanted to wait in case the storm that seems to be hanging out over the summit decides to blow through."

"Are we going to need to pick them up after each weekend? They're made of wood, aren't they? I would think they'd be waterproof."

Tony sat down on the sofa next to me. "I put down frames which the part of the tombstone you can see fits into. I was afraid if we left them unattended for too long, someone might steal them. It won't take long to pick them up at the end of this first weekend and then set them out again for next weekend."

"Did we end up making much money from the idea of selling the tombstones?" I asked, as Tony pulled part of the comforter Tilly and I had been sharing over his lap.

"Over five grand."

My eyes widened. "Five grand? How on earth did you make five grand selling the right to put a personal message on a wooden tombstone?"

Tinder jumped into Tony's lap and began to purr. I suspected that Tang wouldn't be far behind. "I decided to offer a bunch of little tombstones that would allow for a name, a date, and a sentence or two of text, for twenty bucks each. I also built twenty large tombstones that would allow the purchaser to create an extended message, which I sold for a hundred bucks each. Those who bought the large tombstones were mainly businesses wanting to offer sponsorship."

"That's great." I moved to the side when Tang finally joined us. Titan seemed happy laying on top of Tony's feet. "I guess your idea really paid off. I feel like we're as ready as we are ever going to be, but I still feel unsettled."

"It's probably the fact that there have been so many really weird things going on that is causing you anxiety."

I laid my head back down on Tony's shoulder now that everyone was settled. "I will admit that showing up on Monday to find the decorations we'd just hung the day before on the floor, and the walls we'd painted white on Saturday suddenly turned to green by Tuesday, was somewhat disconcerting. To be honest, I think the green walls work better than the white did, but still. How on earth did that happen?"

"I don't know," Tony admitted. "Maybe vandals." He stroked my arm with a finger. "Do you think we should hire someone to provide security at night and on those days the event is closed?"

"Maybe." The warmth from the fire, combined with the body heat created by Tony and I and all the animals, was making me drowsy. "It will be an added expense that will cut into our profit, however, and so far, the vandals, if that is even what is going on, haven't really hurt anything. I guess we should just wait and see how things go once we actually open." I closed my eyes as I struggled to stay awake. "Maybe I should have taken today off just in case there turns out to be a last-minute crisis to see to."

"I'll take care of everything," Tony promised.

"I know you will, and I love you for doing so."

He stood up, picked me up, and carried me back to bed. Titan, Tilly, and the cats followed. After Tony climbed into bed next to me, I curled into the warmth of this man I loved more than life itself. He always knew how to help me to relax and calm my mind. I really don't know how I'd ever gotten by without him.

Chapter 7

"Good morning, Bree," I cheerily greeted my best friend as I dropped off her mail.

"Well, you're certainly in a better mood than I expected."

I rested an elbow on the counter Bree had decorated with fall accents. "Why wouldn't I be in a good mood? The storm that was rumbling over the summit overnight has decided to head north, and it has turned out to be a gorgeous day, everything is ready for opening night tonight, and I am ahead of schedule, so unless something occurs to delay my progress, I might very well get off early."

"I guess you haven't heard."

My smile faded just a bit. "Heard? Heard what?"

Bree hesitated.

"Heard what Bree?"

"I guess maybe I shouldn't have said anything. If Tony didn't call you, he must not have wanted to worry you."

I felt my heart quicken. "What happened to Tony?"

"Tony is fine," Bree assured me. "It's just that he ran into a few problems at the haunted house this morning."

Okay. I could deal with this. "What problems?"

"For one thing, when Tony showed up, the front door was locked. All the doors were locked."

I shrugged. "So? We locked up when we left last night. Tony has a key."

"His key wouldn't work. He had to call a locksmith. Apparently, someone changed all the locks at some point between when you left last night and when Tony arrived this morning."

I frowned. "That's crazy. Who would do such a thing?"

Bree lifted a shoulder. "I don't know. Mike didn't know. It is all rather odd."

"Totally odd. But I suppose that as long as Tony is in now, it isn't a catastrophe."

"There's more," Bree informed me.

I blew out a breath. "Of course, there is. So what else did Tony find when he was finally able to get inside the house?"

"You know those walls downstairs that you painted white that turned green?"

"Yeah."

"They're black now."

"Black?"

She nodded. "Mike says they actually look a lot better, and you probably should have painted them black in the first place. The white would have really stood out under the black light, and the green was a little too green if you know what I mean."

"I guess it is true that black is probably better, but the fact that black is better doesn't really explain the fact that someone broke into the house in the middle of the night, painted all the walls, and then changed the locks before they left."

"That and the whole thing with the bathtub."

I felt the stress in my shoulders begin to build. "What whole thing with the bathtub?"

Bree answered. "I guess someone filled the tub with water that they then died red. Once the tub was full, they put that big skeleton in the hallway into the tub, making it look as if the skeleton was bathing in blood. Mike says it looks cool, and Tony said he'd probably just leave the skeleton where it was, but Tony asked Mike to look into the break-in even though the vandal seemed to have actually improved on things."

I shook my head. "This is really bizarre."

"It is," Bree agreed once again.

"And even if someone thought we should have black walls and a skeleton in a tub of blood, why would they go to all the trouble of changing the locks? How did they change the locks? Did they call a locksmith?"

"Mike told me he checked with the two local locksmiths, but neither one was called out to the house last night. Tony said that the locking mechanism inside the knobs could have been replaced. Seems like a lot of effort to go through just to pull a few pranks if you ask me."

I slid my bag off my shoulder and set it on the floor at my feet. "This whole thing is just so bizarre. Maybe the prankster was in the house for another reason, and the pranks are just a way to distract us from what is really going on."

"Like what?"

I pursed my lips. "I'm not sure. Did anything else other than the paint, locks, and skeleton in the tub happen last night?"

"Well, there was the crying and the water."

"Crying?"

"When Tony finally got inside the house this morning, he heard someone crying. Or at least it sounded like crying. The sound was coming from upstairs, so he went to check it out, but there was no one there, so he went to check in the attic. He didn't find anyone, and the crying had stopped by the time he got there, but he did find a large puddle of water. The water to the house has been turned off since there is a small leak in the basement and the water isn't needed for the event, so Tony had no idea where the water had come from. He followed the wet footprints, but they ended at the wall separating the main body of the attic from the secret room."

Okay, this whole thing was just too bizarre. It sounded like someone was going to a lot of trouble to carry out pranks that were a nuisance but weren't really hurting anything. Who would go to all the trouble? I chatted with Bree for a few more minutes and then continued on my way. I'd lost precious minutes chatting with Bree, so if I did want to get off early, and I did, I'd need to pick up the pace. Still, the fact that someone had broken in and done such odd things had me intrigued. I hadn't delivered the mail to the police station yet. Maybe Mike would be in, and I could get a rational explanation as to what was going on.

"Morning, Frank," I said to Mike's partner. "Is Mike around?"

"In his office."

I bent over to pet Mike's dog, Leonard, who'd come trotting out to greet Tilly and me when he heard my voice. Leonard loved Tilly, so I left them to visit and headed down the hallway.

"I just spoke to Bree," I said, poking my head in through his open door.

"I guess she told you that we had another visit from our prankster last night."

I nodded. "She did. Do you have any idea who might have done such a thing?"

"No idea at all. I checked with every locksmith within a sixty-mile radius, and none admitted to changing the locks on the haunted house. Normally, I'd brush for fingerprints, but half the town has been in that house this week helping to get ready for tonight, so I doubt it would do any good. I did check for prints on the doorknobs, but the only prints I found were Tony's. As you know, the house is very secluded, so I doubt I'll find anyone who saw anything. At least no real damage was done."

"Bree said there was a puddle of water in the attic, but that the water to the house is turned off. How do you explain that?"

"I suppose someone might have brought water up to the attic in a bucket."

"And the wet footprints Tony saw?"

"I guess whoever is responsible for all this, walked through the water, and left the prints."

"Bree said the prints ended at the wall. Where did this person go from there? And how did he disappear without Tony seeing him? He must have still been there when Tony arrived, or the wet prints would have dried."

"I guess he might have gone up that ladder to the clock tower. I'm not sure how he got down from there. Maybe he had a ladder and used it to get down while Tony was calling me. We were on the phone for a good fifteen to twenty minutes discussing the situation before we hung up and Tony went to take another look around."

I supposed all of that made sense. Actually, it made sense from the perspective of how a person would do such a thing, but it didn't make sense from the perspective of why a person would go to so much trouble. Part of me wanted to be angry that someone was messing with us, but another part of me knew that the more odd things that went on, the more people would be hooked into the mystery of the whole thing and the more tickets we'd be able to sell.

Chapter 8

By the time I arrived at the haunted house, the back lot we'd reserved for volunteer parking was close to full indicating to me that most if not all of tonight's volunteers had arrived. I parked near the back of the lot and got out of my Jeep. I'd stopped at home to drop off Tilly and to change out of my uniform, but once I took a minute to stand quietly in the night air, I realized I might not have dressed warm enough.

As I approached the house, I paused to admire Tony's handiwork. The graveyard had been completed, and the tombstones were in place. People were milling around under the lights Tony had hung, reading the inscriptions while waiting for the main attraction to begin. The front door was open, and one of the volunteers was standing by to take tickets and form groups once the clock struck six. Even from the yard, the sounds of thunder, hackling, and screaming could be heard from the sound system. Add in the intentionally flickering lights, and the stage for an evening of horror had been set even before the first mortal was allowed entrance.

"Oh good, you're here," One of the volunteers, a woman named Rayleen Walter, said.

"The place looks great. Are we ready to open?" I asked.

"I think so," Rayleen answered. "Tony is doing a final walkthrough, but the volunteers are all here, and everything seems to be working. Mike said to wait until about five minutes until six to form the first group. Once the tour guide starts, I thought I'd bring in the next group of twenty to wait in the entry."

"Sounds like you have things well in hand."

"I think so. I've had a bunch of people come by wanting to buy tickets, however, and I will admit they aren't happy when they hear the event is sold out. Some of the other volunteers and I were talking about spacing the tours closer together in order to accommodate additional guests. The way it is now, a single group is taken through the entire haunted house before the next group starts. What if we took group one through the first floor and then as soon as they head upstairs, we start group two on the first floor, while group three gathers in the entry."

"Won't the groups collide when group one comes down the stairs just as group two is ready to head up?" I asked.

"Not if you bring the group on the second floor down the back staircase. Sure, it's narrow, and it might be a bit intense if anyone is claustrophobic, but I guess the guides could ask anyone if they would prefer to be escorted out the front. We'll need to steal a few of the volunteers who signed up for other duties to be guides if we are going to bring additional groups through, but in the end, we will make a lot more money, and we will be able to keep those who come by wanting to buy tickets happy."

I paused to consider the idea. "I like your idea, but being a guide requires that the volunteer learn a script. Do we have anyone available who knows the script?"

Rayleen nodded. "Tawny and Valerie both know the script. They are working as floaters tonight, but I bet they'd be happy to do the tours."

"And those who don't want to take the narrow and winding staircase down?"

"I thought we'd use cones to set up a designated area for anyone not comfortable with the back stairs. The tour guide could radio you and let you know we have guests needing an escort, and then you could head up and bring the one or two people who might fall into this category from each group down the main staircase in the front."

I nodded. "Okay. Let's try it. Gather all the tour guides together and tell them to offer a warning to every group that the staircase to exit is steep and narrow and that they can be escorted down the front staircase if they prefer."

"Okay."

"And have the guides call Bree to escort those who choose that option. I want to stay flexible in the event we have any more problems."

"Have Bree set her walkie talkie to channel five, and I'll let the guides know to call her on that channel," Rayleen instructed.

"Okay. I know she's here, so I'll track her down and fill her in."

I smiled as I walked toward the house. If Rayleen's idea worked, that would mean we would be able to sell almost double the number of tickets I'd planned. Now wouldn't that be awesome!

"Looks like the crowd is gathering." Tony walked up behind me and wrapped his arms around my waist.

I took in his scent, leaning back into his chest, and letting his strength help to calm my nerves. "Are we ready?"

"As we'll ever be."

I filled him in on Rayleen's idea to take additional groups through. Tony agreed it was worth trying it out a time or two to see how it went as long as we had additional volunteers who were willing to cover all the shifts. I assured him that Rayleen had assured me that we did.

"I need to talk to Bree, and I want to check in with Mike. Do you know where they are?" I asked.

"The last time I saw Bree, she was upstairs in the second bedroom trying to untangle cobwebs that had fallen, and I think Mike is outside. He said something about walking the perimeter."

I turned in his arms and put my arms around his neck. I reached up, and gave him a quick peck on the lips, before taking a step back. "Okay, I'll head up to talk to Bree first. If you need me. I'll be on channel two, I'm going to have Bree switch to channel five, and I think Mike is on one. The majority of the volunteers with radios are on channel six."

Tony held up his radio. "I'm monitoring channel six, but if I need you, I'll look for you on two."

Tony headed outside to check in with the volunteers who were monitoring the parking area, and I went upstairs to let Bree know about Rayleen's plan.

The first group would be gathering before I knew it, and I wanted to be sure everyone was dialed in before we started bringing guests through. Once I'd caught Bree up with the new plan, I headed outside to find Mike who, along with his rookie, Gage, had volunteered to provide security.

"Have you seen Mike?" I asked one of the volunteers after exiting the house.

"I think he is around back. He mentioned something about looking for a secret entrance."

"Secret entrance?"

"You know these old houses have them. Especially weird old houses like this one. Mike and I were chatting earlier about the fact that Joe had somehow gotten up into the clock tower without having had access to the secret room, and I brought up hidden passages within the walls. Mike wasn't sure this particular house had hidden passages, but I guess I made a good enough argument that he decided to take a look around."

I paused to consider this. "So are you suggesting that the house might have hidden passages like the sort in the movies where a bookcase opens, and a staircase is revealed?"

"Basically. I know it isn't all that usual here in the States, but there are a number of old estates in Europe with hidden passages in the walls. Toured a few in my time."

I sort of doubted that was what was going on here, but I supposed it was possible. After all, the secret room had most likely been there for a long time, and it didn't seem that anyone had noticed it until Tony had realized the roofline looked odd. The house was large, and the rooms were divided up in such a way that figuring out what was on the other side of any of the walls had proven to be a challenge. I thanked the volunteer and then walked around to the back in the hope of finding Mike.

As I rounded the corner, I noticed a shadow cross the attic window. We'd locked the attic since it wasn't part of the tour and we didn't want people messing around up there given the secret room and the unsolved murder. The only people with keys to the attic were Mike, Tony, and me, but maybe Tony had gone up to check the electrical box one last time.

"Did you find the secret passage that I understand you now suspect Joe might have used to access the clock tower on the night he died?" I asked Mike after I found him staring at the exterior staircase that led down to the basement, which we were also not using.

"I haven't. Yet. And I don't know for certain that there is a hidden staircase, but I suppose that it is conceivable that one might be found in a house with both a widow's walk and a clock tower. Whoever designed this place obviously had a taste for the ornamental and unconventional."

"I guess if there is a hidden passage that leads up to the widow's walk, that would explain how Elizabeth came to be up there when she fell. I have been wondering about that. And if a passage likewise exists that leads to the clock tower, that could explain Joe being there. The idea that he climbed up three stories on a ladder to get to the roof to access the tower never really worked for me. Still, I doubt you'll be able to figure it out from out here. Maybe once the haunted house is over and the volunteers have all left, we can take a look around inside."

"That's a good idea. In the meantime, I'll be outside making sure everyone lines up in a polite and organized manner, and that no one parks anywhere except in the area designated for parking. I have a feeling we might have more cars than space."

"I guess the overflow can park on the street. It's a pretty long walk from the street to the house, but it's a nice evening."

Mike nodded. "That could work. I'll have the volunteers monitor the entrance to the parking area so they can let another car in every time someone leaves."

"We do have those spaces in the front that we've set aside for handicap parking as well," I reminded Mike.

"I'll let my guy know. I'll be circulating the parking area and the grounds, so if anything comes up, just let me know."

"I'm on two," I informed Mike. "Bree is on five, and Tony is on six along with the other volunteers."

"Okay. I'll monitor all the channels."

The next few hours went by quickly. So far, everything had gone smoothly, and only a handful of people had requested to be escorted down the main staircase. It almost seemed as if the others enjoyed the creep factor of the back staircase, which did have a feel to it that seemed to mimic the narrow staircases found in old manors. While a majority of the home was constructed of wood, the back staircase, as well as the grand entry and the widow's walk, had been constructed of stone. I found this interesting in and of itself.

"Is Shaggy still around?" One of the volunteers who'd been helping with the props, sound effects, and lighting asked.

"He should be. Is there a problem?" I asked.

"The lid on the coffin in the second bedroom on the second floor is supposed to go up and down, but it is stuck in an upward position. It's not a huge problem. There is a vampire inside, and it still makes a creaking noise and looks spooky, but I figured that if Shaggy is around, you might want him to take a look at it before he leaves."

"I'll find him and let him know," I promised. "How is everything else doing?"

"Good. We had a problem with the lights in the chamber of torture on the first floor right after opening, but Tony seems to have them working again. I'm actually sort of surprised that the electrical system in this old house can handle all these props."

"We had the primary circuit board updated, and we added a second board for the props. It was a bit of an expense, but we wanted to be able to provide the ultimate experience, so the upgrade was necessary." I looked toward the entrance. It appeared as if the crowd was thinning. "I'm going to go and find Shaggy, and then take a look outside. Will you be here tomorrow?"

"I'll be here."

"Awesome. Thank you for all the time you've put in."

I found Shaggy just as he was getting ready to head out, and told him about the malfunctioning coffin. He told me that he'd come by and fix it in the morning since tonight's event was coming to a close and he had a date. I agreed that that was fine. I checked in with the parking crew and was informed that everyone was filing out in an orderly fashion and that they didn't expect any problems. Then, I went and looked for Mike to let him know that the volunteer crew would be gone in about an hour, and once they were gone, we could begin looking for the secret passage. I walked one of the volunteers, a grandmother named Gloria, out to her car and it was during our walk that I stumbled across the first real clue as to what might have occurred on the night Joe died.

"I was chatting with Gloria as I walked her out to her car, and she swears that she saw Joe up on the widow's walk on the day he came to volunteer with Grange," I said to Bree, Mike, and Tony after everyone else had left. "She said she was heading out to her car after most everyone else had left and saw him standing up there. She thought it was odd, but she knew he was a contractor, so she figured he had a good reason to be up there. Like maybe, something needed repair. She never mentioned it to anyone since she didn't think it was relevant, but then when I was chatting with her tonight, she told me she had been thinking about it since she found out that Joe's body was found in the clock tower, and wanted to mention it."

"And she has no idea why he was up there other than her assumption that he was repairing something?" Mike asked.

"She said he was looking over the railing, so it entered her mind that perhaps he was repairing the railing, but she didn't know for certain."

"So how did he get up there?" Bree asked.

"Mike and I think there might be secret passages hidden in the walls of the house," I answered.

Tony slowly bobbed his head. "I've been looking at the walls and how their placement interacts with the roofline ever since we found the secret room. I think there might have been stairs connecting the landing on the second floor to the widow's walk and clock tower via the back staircase at one time. The wall is really wide in this area as if a staircase once existed but was removed or walled in."

"Maybe Edward walled it in after Elizabeth fell to her death," I suggested.

"If she fell and wasn't pushed," Bree added.

"I assumed the wall was solid," Tony continued, "but maybe it isn't. Maybe there is a trick to accessing the space via a moving panel in either the second-floor hallway or the attic."

It was at this point that the four of us headed for the stairs. Tony suggested starting with an access point from the end of the existing staircase. Currently, the narrow stairs led to a small landing which featured a closet that might have been designated for linens on the back wall. If you turned right at the top of the stairs, you could access the second-floor rooms. If at some point the staircase had continued on to the widow's walk and clock tower, it would have been located where the closet now existed. Tony and Mike set to work to try to find the lever that would open the wall assuming one actually existed.

"I think I have something," Mike said after a good twenty minutes of us tapping on the walls, pushing on shelves, and looking for any sort of lever or knob. Bree, Tony, and I gathered behind Mike as he pushed one of the shelves to the side, and the wall opened, revealing a wooden staircase.

"Well, look at that," Bree said.

The staircase was narrow and steep and led straight up toward another wall. Eventually, Mike found the lever to open that wall as well. The opening led out to the widow's walk. There a narrow ledge which led from the widow's walk to the clock tower. "I think we know how Joe and his killer got up here," Mike said.

"I think you might be right." I pointed to the dusty steps. "Footprints. And not just yours."

Chapter 9

Saturday, October 19

I reached out to find the bed empty beside me. Slowly opening my eyes, I looked toward the window to find the sun high in the sky. It had been late by the time we'd gotten back to my cabin last night, and I hadn't slept well the night before, so once my head hit the pillow, I was out like a light. I considered pulling the covers over my head and going back to sleep, but I could smell bacon and coffee that seemed to accompany the sounds coming from the kitchen, and I figured bacon and coffee were worth getting up for. I glanced over the side of the bed to see that even Tilly had deserted me. Not that I blamed her. As I'd already established, bacon and coffee were a heck of a good reason to pull ones tired body out of bed.

Tugging on my robe, I headed toward the kitchen, a short journey in my little cabin. "Wow, what's all of this?"

Tony handed me a cup of coffee already splashed with cream. "We never did eat dinner last night, and I suspect we won't be having much of a dinner tonight, so I decided to make a big breakfast to tide us over. How do you want your eggs?"

I looked at the muffins, home fries, bacon, and sausage already on the table. "Scrambled is fine." I really didn't see how we were ever going to eat all this food, but I was committed to doing my part in the effort.

"So what time did you want to head over to the haunted house?" Tony asked, refilling my coffee.

"It opens at six, and the volunteers are due to arrive at five, so I'd like to be there by four at the latest. Maybe even earlier just in case our prankster has been busy and has locked us out again."

"I sort of doubt that whoever is pranking us would pull the same prank twice, but I get what you are saying." Tony poured the eggs he'd beaten into a pan.

"Was there something specific you wanted to do today before we have to head over to the house?" I asked, as I broke a muffin in half and buttered one side.

"I've been thinking about the hidden staircase and the fact that Joe must have found it, which is how he came to be in the clock tower when he died. It occurred to me we might want to have a heart to heart with Grange. I mean Joe and Grange had been friends and coworkers before Joe went solo, and Joe did come to the house in the first place at Grange's invitation. I think he might know something we don't about Joe's motivation for returning to the house that night."

I took a bite of the muffin I'd just buttered. "Okay, so do you want to stop by Grange's house later?"

"I called Grange, and he is taking his boys to the fishing derby they are holding out at the apple farm today. He said if we wanted to stop by, he would be happy to chat with us."

The Harlow Family Apple Farm was a well-known fall destination in the area. Not only did they sell everything apples, including pick your own apples and apple pie, but they had a pumpkin patch, hay maze, and fishing pond as well.

"Okay," I said. "That could actually be fun. I'll get ready as soon as we eat. I don't think they allow dogs, so I guess we should walk the kids before we go."

"I took the dogs for a walk while you were sleeping. They should be fine until we get home."

"And the cats? Have they been fed?"

"All the animals have been fed. Do you want orange juice or just coffee?"

"Just coffee."

After taking a minute to fill my plate with the delicious food Tony had made, I sat back to consider the situation. "I've been thinking about the fact that it looks as if Joe found the hidden passage that led to the widow's walk, but how did he know it was there in the first place?"

"I'm not sure. I'm hoping Grange might know. We didn't talk long when I called him this morning, but he did say that one of the reasons he approached Joe about helping out with the repairs on the house in spite of the fact that he really isn't a dog person who would think to volunteer for a shelter fundraiser is because he has been interested in the house for a long time and figured he would welcome the opportunity to get a peek inside.

"So maybe he knew something about the history of the place before he even showed up to work."

"That would be my guess. I don't know to what extent he'd studied the history of the house, but perhaps Grange will know."

"Perhaps. By the way, Shaggy is going fix a malfunctioning coffin this morning. Do you know if he has a key to the place? If not, we'll need to go by to let him in."

"He doesn't have a key. We talked about it last night, and he decided to show up early for his shift this evening. He said he'd be there no later than four. We should be there by then, so we can let him in, and I can give him a hand if need be."

"He really has done a great job with the props. Sometimes I forget that behind the childlike exterior is a pretty smart guy."

"He is smart. But I know what you are saying. He does have a quality about him that makes one wonder if he isn't a perpetual child."

In spite of the massive quantity of food Tony had prepared, we actually managed to do a pretty good job finishing it off. He really was a good cook, and I enjoyed the meals he prepared. Having a huge breakfast would not keep me away from the apple fritters at the apple farm. Eating everything apple during the fall was a long-held tradition in the Thomas family.

After we arrived and parked, we headed toward the fishing pond which is where Grange had told Tony he'd be. I hoped we'd have time to pick some apples and maybe gather a few pumpkins before we had to leave since being at the farm had put me in the mood to do both. I remembered coming here with Mike and my mom and my dad when I was a kid. Every year we'd taken a full day to enjoy all that the farm had to offer. At some point, we'd stopped coming. I supposed it was after my dad died, or at least after we'd been informed of his death despite his very undead state of being.

"I forgot how much I loved coming here," I said to Tony as we walked hand in hand across the well-groomed lawn toward the fishing pond. It was nice being in the midst of families enjoying the perfect autumn day. Kids ran in every direction playing games of tag, while their parents sat on blankets in the shade sharing a bottle of apple wine. When was the last time Tony and I had sat and simply relaxed? It seemed that as of late when I wasn't delivering mail, and he wasn't working with his software customers, he was working on his video game with Shaggy, and I was either volunteering at the shelter or at one of the multitudes of community events the town held.

"There he is," Tony pointed toward a picnic table where Grange was sitting with another man about his age watching a group of kids fish.

"Tess, Tony," Grange greeted as we walked up. "This is my friend, Bob."

"Happy to meet you," Tony and I both responded.

"Pull up a seat," Grange offered.

Tony and I sat down on the bench across from him.

"I'm going to go into town and get some more bait like we discussed," Bob informed Grange. "Do you want me to get more beer as well?"

"Always."

Once Bob left, Tony got right to the point. "As I indicated when I called, we wanted to talk to you about Joe and his relationship with the Vandenberg house. We figure that if we can find out the reason he went back that night, we might be able to track down his killer."

"I'm happy to share what I know," Grange answered. "Joe was a good guy. I want his killer brought to justice."

"As do we," I agreed.

He cleared his throat. "I guess Joe first found out about the house three or four years ago. He was still working for Greg and me then, and we had this kitchen remodel just outside of town. Joe and I live in the same neighborhood, so we'd carpool to and from work. The job took us past the Vandenberg house each day, and it seemed like we'd end up talking about it. Joe was fascinated by the architecture. I'd actually studied architecture before deciding to go into construction with my dad and brother, so while I didn't finish college, I knew enough to make the conversation interesting."

"It certainly is an interesting house," Tony said. "What exactly would you call that style?"

"Early American Hodgepodge," Grange chuckled.

"It is eclectic," I agreed.

"I know that Edward Vandenberg was from England," Grange said. "He came from a wealthy family, and he used his inheritance to come to the States and make a name for himself. He settled in the area early in its history and was actually one of the first men to own and operate a lumber mill. He didn't stay, so he isn't considered to be a town founder, but he was influential in the development of what was to come after."

"And Elizabeth?" I asked.

"She was English as well. I guess she came to the area to be with Edward. They married but never had children. And as you know, she fell to her death from the widow's walk. Edward eventually married a woman named Barbara, and they had one child, a girl named Ethel. Barbara fell down the stairs and broke her neck. At some point after that, Edward went back to England, and Ethel lived in the house alone."

I raised a brow. "I thought Edward died."

"Not as far as I know. I did a bit of research at one point, and I never found evidence of his death. I did find a news article where Ethel told the reporter that her dad had moved back to England, although she didn't elaborate as to when or why he returned and left her alone in the house."

"Was she an adult by this point?" I asked.

"A young adult. I'd say early thirties, although I'm uncertain as to the exact year."

I glanced at Tony. His expression was thoughtful.

"So the dad moves away, and Ethel lives alone in the house for the rest of her life?" I asked.

"As far as I know," Grange answered. "I really have no idea why she never married, but I was never able to find any sort of evidence that she had, so I have to assume she hadn't."

"The widow's walk looked as if it was added to the structure for ornamental reasons. Did you know there was a hidden passage that would allow access?" I asked Grange.

"Did I know there was one? No. Did I suspect there was one? Yes. On many occasions, Joe and I discussed that it made no sense to build a widow's walk and clock tower and not include a means of accessing them. We both suspected that Edward walled in the access to the stairs leading up to the roof area after Elizabeth fell. I wouldn't be at all surprised if Joe went back to the house to look for the access. He was even more fascinated in the mystery surrounding the Vandenberg house than I was. I was curious, but at times, I was convinced that Joe was obsessed."

"As it turns out, there is a hidden passage, and it does appear that someone, probably Joe, found it," Tony said. "I guess if Joe was as fascinated with the mystery as you say, it is conceivable that he unlatched a window so he could get back in to take a look around after everyone had left, and if he found the hidden passage, it makes sense he might have used it to check out the clock tower. What we don't know is who killed him. Joe must have had someone with him. Any idea who?"

Grange paused. He tilted his head and drummed his fingers on the table in front of him. "Honestly, if Joe did have plans to go back and look for the hidden passage, I'm surprised he didn't call me. We'd talked about it often enough, and even though some people assume we had a falling out since he went into business for himself, nothing could be further from the truth. Joe and I have been friends for a long time. I understood his desire to have his own business. I felt the same way when I decided to work for my dad instead of pursuing a career as an architect. In spite of what others have said, the two of us were fine. Good even. There isn't a single reason I can think of why he would have called anyone other than me to go on this adventure with him if that is what he planned to do."

"And yet, that seems to be exactly what he did. If not you, who do you think he would be most likely to ask?"

Grange slowly shook his head. "I really don't know. Maybe his neighbor. I think his name is Jack. The two weren't close the way Joe and I were close, but their wives are friends, and I know they barbecue and hang out from time to time. I suppose the two men might have chatted about the house at some point along the line, and if they did, Joe might have thought to include Jack in his treasure hunt."

"Treasure hunt?" I asked. "Are you talking about a real treasure as in money and jewels and treasure like that?"

Grange nodded. "Like I said, Edward was a rich man from a rich family. It is a well-held belief that he brought his millions to America with him. Some people say that Edward took his riches home with him when he left and returned to England, and others say he was murdered and never left, and that the riches he brought to America with him are still hidden somewhere in that house."

Chapter 10

"Well, the rumor about a treasure certainly lends itself to an interesting twist to this story," I said to Tony as we headed back toward my cabin.

"It certainly does. It would seem a treasure worth millions might be a pretty good motive for murder."

"So are we thinking that perhaps Joe and Jack were participating in a neighborhood barbecue and somehow they got on the subject of the Vandenberg house? The men began to talk, theories were shared, and after a few beers, Joe finds himself telling Jack about the treasure that is rumored to be hidden somewhere in the house. When Grange offers Joe the opportunity to get a peek inside the house as a volunteer, he takes it. He has a look around and notices the odd roofline the same as you did. Being a contractor, he suspects a secret room or passage of some sort. The place is packed with volunteers, so he unlatches a window and plans to return later. He waits for his wife to go to bed and then sneaks out. Either he knows he'll need help and hits up the neighbor, or the neighbor sees him leaving and asks him about it. One way or another, they both end up at the house. They find the secret staircase leading to the widow's walk. Once they have accessed the widow's walk, they realize they can also access the clock tower. They do so and then Jack, figuring that if Joe is dead, he can have the treasure to himself, kills Joe and leaves him where he is certain that no one will find him."

Tony adjusted his hands on the wheel. "That all fits, but why kill Joe? I sort of doubt they found the treasure in the small amount of time they might have been at the house. Why kill him at that point?"

"Maybe Jack assumed that Joe was the only one who knew about the treasure and he didn't want to risk him telling someone else," I said, but I was actually less than sure of this.

"I guess we should call Mike when we get back and let him sort this out."

"Yeah," I sighed, feeling down about not being there for the kill. "I guess that would be best. Mike can talk to Jack, and if he is guilty, he can arrest him. You and I have a fundraiser to prepare for."

By the time we returned to the cabin, called Mike, and filled him in on everything we knew as well as everything we suspected, we barely had time to grab a light lunch and head to the haunted house. Neither of us had reason to believe the pranksters had struck again, but they'd been making regular appearances to this point, so we figured it was prudent to be better safe than sorry.

As it turned out, we were glad we'd arrived at three instead of four since it looked as if the prankster had struck again during the overnight hours.

"I don't get it," I said, staring at the house on which someone had painted red tears dripping down from the upstairs windows. It looked as if the house was crying blood.

"It's just someone needing to leave their mark." Tony looked at the house. "I have time to paint over it if you want. The paint won't have time to dry, but the tears are on the exterior of the house so it should be fine."

"Let's look inside first to make sure we don't have an even a bigger issue to deal with in there."

Thankfully, the interior of the house was undisturbed, so Tony and I went back to deal with the tears.

"I can paint over the red paint with white paint, but the exterior of the house is so dilapidated and the paint so worn, that the white paint is going to stand out as much as the red does now. I certainly don't have time to paint the entire house to blend in the white I was going to add to cover the red. What do you want to do?" Tony asked.

"It's sort of creepy, but I guess it works okay given our theme. Just leave it the way it is. We don't have time to fix it. It will be almost dark by the time everyone shows up, so it isn't like it is going to stand out. I guess if we decide we need to cover it, we can tackle it tomorrow."

"Okay. That sounds like a good plan." Tony looked toward the house. "Now that I know about the treasure, I can't help wondering about it."

"You know what I'm wondering? I'm wondering if our skeleton in the secret room isn't actually Edward Vandenberg."

Tony raised a brow. "You think?"

"Grange didn't know for certain what had become of the man," I pointed out. "He said he couldn't find anything to verify his death here in the States, but I wonder if he checked for a death certificate in England."

"I guess it might be worth looking into," Tony agreed. "If we are unable to find proof that he actually returned to England, then the theory of the body in the secret room being Edward does make sense."

"Didn't Mike describe him as a cruel and abusive father? Maybe Ethel took matters into her own hands," I suggested.

"It is a story that works. We'll do some digging tomorrow. Right now, we have a fundraiser to pull off. Are we going to do the extra groups again tonight?" Tony asked.

I shrugged. "I guess so if we have enough volunteers to lead the extra groups. It seemed to work fine last night, and it did allow us to make a lot of extra money for the animals."

"We should go ahead and schedule extra volunteers for next weekend and Halloween," Tony suggested. "I guess this weekend we'll just work with what we have and take as many ticket-buying spectators through as we can. I have a feeling that now that we're open, people are going to start showing up in droves."

"If we really want to bring in the customers, we should leak the rumor about the hidden treasure."

"I don't think that would bring in ticket buyers. What I think it would do is bring unwanted trespassers," Tony pointed out.

"I guess you have a point. Maybe we should keep the rumor about the treasure between you and me and Mike and Grange for now. And Bree, of course. I doubt the dang thing really exists, but wouldn't it be something if it did? We could build a palace for unwanted animals if we found a treasure worth millions."

"If it does exist, and I sort of doubt it does, I'm afraid it would belong to the current owner of the house and not to us even if we found it," Tony informed me.

I supposed Tony was right. A palace for unwanted animals would be fun, but at this point, I'd settle for the house we'd originally envisioned.

Chapter 11

Sunday, October 20

"Brady is calling for you on the house line," Tony called up the stairs to me. We'd decided to come out to his place after we left the haunted house last evening, so I had to wonder why Brady was calling on Tony's home line rather than my cell. I picked up my cell and noticed the three missed calls. Ah, I guess that was why.

"Hey, Brady, what's up?" I asked after answering.

"I need your help if you are available this morning."

"I can be. What do you need?"

"Susan Wallaby called to let me know that she was out walking her dog when she came across a mama cat with a brand new litter of kittens. She said she would have trapped and transported them herself, but she'd noticed a pair of coyotes lurking nearby, so she didn't want to leave the kittens while she went home to get a cat carrier. She called me from her cell and asked if I would come out and pick them up. I would, but I have a dog in my operating room that has been hit by a car and needs stitches. I was hoping you could help Susan out."

"I can and will. Where are they?"

Brady gave me Susan's location and her cell number. I pulled on tennis shoes and headed down the stairs. "I need to go pick up a feral cat and her kittens who are being stalked by coyotes. Do you want to come?"

"Yeah, I'll come," Tony answered. "Just let me grab my wallet and keys."

"While you're doing that, I'll run out to the garage and grab a trap. I think I left one here after the raccoon incident. I'll meet you by the truck."

The trap I had was a large animal carrier with a door that you could set to close automatically after the animal you were trying to trap walked in. It was perfect for capturing raccoons in need of relocation or feral cats with new babies who might otherwise be uncatchable. I'd first brought the crate to Tony's after a raccoon had gotten into his house through an open door and refused to leave. It had taken two days to catch the little trespasser, but we were eventually able to safely relocate him to the forest where he belonged.

"Do you have everything you need?" Tony asked after arriving at the truck and unlocking the doors.

"I do. Luckily, Susan lives on this end of town, so the location she told us to meet her is only about ten minutes from here."

Once we arrived at the river where Susan had been walking, she led us to a drainage pipe. The kittens were in too far to simply reach in and grab, so it looked like belly crawling through the mud was going to be in my future. I would go in first followed by Tony, whom I would pass the kittens back to one at a time, then he would hand them to Susan, who would place them in the crate which we'd prepared with a warm blanket ahead of time. Once all the kittens were removed, we'd place the trap near the entrance and wait for the mama cat whom we were sure would take off the moment we approached. It was a plan that had worked many times in the past. I just hoped it worked this time. There was always the risk that the mama cat would simply take off and abandon her babies.

Once all five of the babies were safely in the crate, I set the trap door feature, and then Susan, Tony, and I hid behind a rock outcropping waiting for the mama cat. The babies were making a whole lot of noise, so I just hoped mama would show up before the coyotes who were still lurking nearby decided to take a chance and make a move for their breakfast even though humans were hanging around.

"Thanks for coming," Susan said, in a tone barely above a whisper after we settled in to wait. "I wasn't sure what to do. I knew if I left, the coyotes would get the kittens before I could make it back with a way to transport them."

"I'm glad you called," I whispered back. "And thank you for staying to watch over the little guys. I think you're right about the coyotes."

"Did you see where the mama went?" Tony asked after a few minutes. Waiting for the mama to come back for the babies was always nerve-racking.

"No, but I doubt she went far. Are the coyotes still lingering beyond the gully?"

Tony stood up, looked around, and then crouched back down. "They moved further into the woods once we arrived, but they're still there. I hope the mama cat doesn't wander too far away."

I swallowed hard. "Yeah, me too."

"I wanted to tell you that I really enjoyed the haunted house last night," Susan said while we waited for the mama cat to make her move. "I'm actually volunteering tonight, but I attended last night with my cousins who were in town. We all had a blast. Everything turned out perfectly."

"Everyone who has volunteered has done a wonderful job," I answered. "I really think we are going to make more than enough to get started on the expansion."

"That's fantastic. You and Brady have really done so much for the homeless animals in our area. I can't tell you how much we all appreciate it."

I smiled.

"Oh look, there's the mother," Susan whispered.

We watched in silence as she approached the crate, looked around suspiciously, and then circled several times, calling out to her babies the entire time. She eventually entered the crate, and the door closed behind her as it was designed to do. Brady had a nursery all set up at the shelter for new mamas and their babies, so we planned to take them there. Once the babies were weaned, we'd spay and neuter them, then find homes for the kittens and the mama. If she was too wild to be happy in a domesticated situation, we'd make a home for her at the shelter.

"I've been in that house once before," Susan said as we walked back toward the road where Tony had parked.

"The haunted house?" I asked.

She nodded. "When I was a kid. My friend, Trent, knew of a way to get in. By that point, the people who lived there had moved, and no one had lived there for a few years, so Trent convinced me and a couple of his other friends to break in so we could help him look for the treasure."

"Treasure?" So there were others who knew the rumor.

Susan nodded. "Trent said that the first guy who lived in the house brought gold and jewels and stuff with him when he moved here. Trent said the treasure was hidden somewhere in the house, but no one knew about it, so no one had gone looking for it."

"How did Trent know about it?" I asked.

"I'm not a hundred percent sure, but I think one of his friends heard about the treasure from an uncle or something. Anyway, I guess there is this big gas heater in the basement. A really old one. And since gas can be toxic, the heater is vented. Trent knew about the vent, which had a screen over it that was secured with a lock, and was a large enough opening to crawl through. Trent brought bolt cutters, and after he cut the lock, we opened the screen and crawled through. Once we were inside, we looked around, but we didn't find the treasure. Trent thought it was hidden inside one of the walls, but none of us wanted to get in trouble, so when he suggested coming back with a sledgehammer to open up the walls, the rest of us declined."

"Did Trent ever go back?" I asked as we arrived at the truck and Tony opened the back door to strap the carrier in.

"I don't know. If he did, he didn't find the treasure, that's for sure. Trent is as broke as he ever was."

"He still lives in town?"

Susan nodded. "He's a lifer, like me. You might have met him. He works as an electrician. I remember seeing him at the house early on, right after you started fixing it up. I was coming, and he was going."

"Tall guy? Thin? Dark hair and bushy eyebrows?" I asked.

Susan nodded. "That would be Trent."

I did remember him. He came out twice to look at the electrical. The second time he was out, I asked Joe to show him where the outlet that needed repair was located. The men seemed to know each other. If they both knew about the supposed treasure, could they have stopped to talk about it? I had to wonder if that discussion had led to whatever happened later that led to Joe's death.

Chapter 12

Tony and I met Mike and Bree at a resort out on White Eagle Lake which was known for its Sunday brunch. Most weeks, we all went to Mom's for a meal after church, but this Sunday with the fundraiser and all the extra work we had to do, supper at Mom's had been canceled. Mom was a stickler for attending services, but Mike, Bree, Tony, and I decided to have brunch instead.

"I'm glad you were able to save the baby kittens," Bree said. "Are they going to be okay?"

"Brady said that the mom and babies all seem to be perfectly healthy," I answered. "It's a good thing Susan found them when she did. Those coyotes looked pretty determined to start the day off with a brunch of their own."

Bree made a face. "I know that coyotes have to eat, but I'd just as soon not think about it."

I couldn't agree more. I turned to Mike. "So did you have a chance to speak to Joe's neighbor, Jack?"

"I did. He admitted that he and Joe had discussed the house and the treasure in the past, but he was out of town on the night that Joe died, so he couldn't have been the one to kill him. Too bad. He made a good suspect."

"I might have another one," I responded and proceeded to tell Mike what Susan had told me about Trent. The fact that he knew about the alleged treasure, how to get into the house, and seemed to know Joe, made him a real candidate in my book.

Mike frowned. "I know Trent. I really don't see him being a killer."

I lifted a shoulder. "And maybe he isn't. Still, it might not hurt to speak to him. If he didn't kill Joe, maybe Joe mentioned something to him that will help us figure out who might have met Joe at the house the night he died."

"I'll talk to him," Mike answered. "I really don't think Trent did it, but you are correct in that he might know something." Mike took a bite of his egg, chewing slowly before he swallowed. "Do you remember if Trent volunteered on the day Joe died?"

"Yes, that was the day I asked Joe to show Trent where the outlet in need of repair was. I'm pretty sure that day, the day Joe died, was the only day Joe was at the house."

"So it does stand to reason that they could have prearranged to meet back at the house after everyone left," Tony said. "If they both knew about the treasure and if they both were interested in it, they might have discussed it at some point." Mike turned his attention to his plate. "Has anyone tried the salmon?"

The conversation took a meandering path at this point and eventually settled on the upcoming Thanksgiving holiday.

"Mike and I would really like to host Thanksgiving at our place this year, but when I mentioned it to your mother, she sort of frowned, and said she'd need to think about it," Bree said to me. "I realize that your mom usually cooks the Thanksgiving dinner, but this is our first year as a married couple, and we really want to host. Don't we, dear?"

"Uh, yeah, sure," Mike replied.

"I know it is important to Mom to host the holidays," I said to Bree. "And up to this point, she hasn't had to compete with anyone for the right to do so, but I understand where you are coming from as well. I'm sure there will be a period of adjustment now that there are two Thomas women who like to cook, so maybe you can sit down with Mom and talk about it. Maybe you can cook the meal together, or maybe one of you can host Thanksgiving, and the other one can do Christmas. You did work together well last Thanksgiving when we were at the lake."

"Maybe we should just go to the lake again," Mike suggested. "That way, the question of which house to host the meal in won't come into play and a few days of fishing sounds just about perfect to me. With Gage on board, I should be able to work it out to have some time off."

"I guess that could be an option you might want to bring up with Mom." I looked at Tony. "Do you care one way or another if we go to the lake or are here in White Eagle over the holiday?"

"Either is fine with me."

I smiled at my man. He was always so easy to get along with. Mike and Bree could both be bullheaded at times, but Tony was about as easy going as a man could be.

"Mom and Aunt Ruthie closed the restaurant over Thanksgiving last year," I reminded everyone. "If we went to the lake again, Aunt Ruthie would need to be part of the discussion. Maybe we should all discuss it as a family rather than putting it on Bree to work it out with Mom." I looked at Bree. "If Mom is okay with a lake trip, would you be okay with not hosting at your house?"

She looked at Mike. I could see that she was conflicted. She blew out a breath. "I guess that would be okay. It was fun being at the lake last year. Maybe this year we won't have to spend all our time trying to solve a murder."

"I'm sure the odds are in our favor that we won't," Mike said.

"I'm wondering if we should plan a trip to a different lake given Dad's connection to the lake we visited last year," I suggested. "I know it was Mom's idea to visit the lake in the first place, but she might not want to be weighed down with a reminder of what she's lost again this year."

"Grizzly Lake has that new resort," Bree said. "They have a lodge, but they also have cabins. It would be nice if each couple had their own cabin instead of sharing like we did last year."

"Of course, then Mom would be alone," I pointed out.

"Maybe Aunt Ruthie would want to come along," Mike suggested.

I sort of doubted it, but maybe.

"I'll approach Mom with the idea this week and see how she responds," I offered, realizing after thinking about it that my approaching Mom alone would most likely be the path of least resistance. "We can discuss it in more depth after I see how that goes."

Everyone agreed to the plan, and the discussion looped back around to the bodies we'd found at the haunted house.

"I've been thinking about the concept that the skeleton in the closet is actually the long-deceased Edward Vandenberg," Mike said. "I'm struggling with a way to prove or disprove it." He looked at Tony. "Any ideas?"

"Maybe a forensic anthropologist? I know a guy who should be able to tell you if the skeleton you have could have been Edward Vandenberg. I'll call him and see if he has time to take a look."

"Thanks. I appreciate that. I guess at this point, I'm going to focus my attention on figuring out who killed Joe Brown. At least his death is recent enough to make finding the killer doable."

"Did you ever figure out how he got in?" Bree asked.

"Not really," Mike replied. "We suspect he left a window unlatched when he was at the house volunteering that day. Once inside, we are assuming he found the secret staircase and then used it to access the clock tower. We don't know why he wanted to access the clock tower or who he was with, but perhaps he believed the treasure he was looking for was hidden up there."

"Do you think there really is a treasure?"

"Probably not," Mike answered Bree's question. "If Edward Vandenberg did go back to England, chances are he took whatever wealth he'd brought to the States with him, and if it does turn out that he ended up encased in the secret room Tony found, then chances are his daughter used the money to live off of. I haven't found any sort of documentation to show that she had a means of gainful employment once her father left and the mill was shut down."

"It is sort of odd that Ethel lived all alone in that house for so many years," I added. "Are we sure she never married or took in a roommate?"

"Not that I've been able to find," Mike assured me. "As far as I can tell, Ethel lived with her father until he either returned to England or died and then she lived alone until she died in nineteen sixty at the age of forty-nine."

"And how did she die?"

"No one knows for certain. She was found dead in her home after the man who maintained her septic system had been unable to reach her and had eventually notified law enforcement. The cause of death appeared to have been natural, but was never conclusively determined."

"Natural?" I asked. "As in a heart attack, stroke, or something like that?"

Mike nodded. "There was no sign of forced entry or trauma to the body, which might indicate an assault or an accident. Unfortunately, Ethel had been dead for several months before her body was discovered, so any evidence as to how she died was compromised by that point."

I wrinkled my nose. "The poor woman. To have died all alone in that big old house with no one around to even know what had happened."

"I'm afraid the house saw nothing but tragedy from the moment Edward built it and brought Elizabeth to live there," Mike said.

Chapter 13

Tuesday, October 22

Tony was able to arrange for his forensic friend to look at the bones we'd found in the secret room and tell us what he could about them. He worked out of a lab in DC, so Tony had called his friend with the private jet and made arrangements to accompany the bones, which Mike had released into Tony's care, to the lab. In trade for his friend's time with the skeleton, Tony had agreed to take care of some upgrades his friend wanted to do to his computer system, so he arranged to spend two nights in DC. Tony promised he'd be back on Thursday in plenty of time to help with the fundraiser this weekend, but in the meantime, I was on my own. Tony had always traveled a lot for work, so you would think I would be used to his absences, but when I returned home to my cabin to find only the animals to keep me company, I realized I was really going to miss him.

Normally, I would have called Bree and suggested we get together for a drink, but she was a married woman now who usually had plans with Mike. Tony really hadn't worked out of town much since he'd made the decision to work with Shaggy on the game they were developing, but if he did decide to go back to frequent traveling at some point, I supposed I'd need to make a new friend.

After deciding to scramble an egg for dinner, I poured myself a glass of wine and settled onto the living room sofa.

The discussion Tony, Mike, Bree, and I'd had at brunch on Sunday had gotten me thinking about my father. When I'd briefly seen him in March, he'd asked me to stop looking for him. He'd told me that by doing so, I would not only be putting him in danger, but Mike, Mom, and myself as well. After all the lies he'd told to disappear in the first place, I still found that I believed him, so I stopped all the tracking and computer searches Tony had been conducting and decided to simply let him go.

Of course, that didn't mean that I didn't think about him from time to time. I guess it had been a while, but talking about the lake where he'd gone fishing every Thanksgiving had brought up a lot of memories. Tony and I were the only ones who knew the entire story relating to my father, but I'd shared enough with Mike to cause him to be curious, and every now and then, he brought up the fact that one of these days he was going to take the time to really look for the man.

I never should have told Mike what I knew. Dad wanted to be dead. I should have let him remain dead, at least as far as Mike was concerned.

I got up from the sofa where Tang and Tinder were competing to sit the closest to me and grabbed an old photo album that I'd left on the shelf. There were photos of Mom, Dad, Mike, and me from when Mike and I were kids. Dad hadn't always been the best dad. In fact, most of the time, he was an absent dad, but I'd loved him, and I knew he loved Mike and me. He was away more than he was home, but when he was home, he did things for us such as teaching us to ride a bike, taking us to the lake, or simply hanging out in the yard and tossing a ball around.

To find out all these years later that he'd been living a secret life the entire time he was masquerading as our dad, was still something I had a hard time wrapping my mind around.

I smiled as I flipped through the pages of the old album. In spite of everything, we'd had a good childhood. Mom had been a wonderful and caring parent who was there for all the moments of our lives even if Dad hadn't always been around. I thought about Bree and her desire to establish a place in the Thomas family hierarchy. Mom had always been the only Mrs. Thomas in the family since Dad didn't have a mom, or at least he didn't have a mom we'd ever met. Mom loved to cook, and cooking for the entire Thomas family had always been one of the things she'd done to demonstrate her love for us. I hated to cook, so Mom had no competition from me on that count, but Bree, like Mom, loved to mess around in the kitchen. I sensed that the potential for a real struggle between the two might be lurking in the background if they didn't work out a compromise. Thanksgiving might represent the first tiny battle, but I could see Bree wanting to host Sunday dinners and even family birthdays as time went on.

I closed the photo album and put it back on the shelf. The last thing I wanted to do was get in the middle of a power struggle between the two. I knew that Mom loved Bree and wanted her to be happy, so maybe she'd willingly give up some of her well-established ground to the new woman in her son's life.

Pouring a second glass of wine, I logged onto my computer. I checked my emails, most of which were spam. Logging off, I decided that what I really needed was to expend some energy, so I tossed a log on the fire and headed out to take Tilly and Titan for a walk. The air was crisp, and the sun had set, although it wasn't completely dark yet. I grabbed a flashlight just to be safe and headed down the narrow woodland trail that wound through the forest. I loved being outdoors at this time of the year. The smell of smoke from my wood fire filled the air as leaves fell gently to the ground all around me. I zipped up my sweatshirt against the chill as the sky grew dark. After only a half a mile, I turned around and headed back toward my cabin.

"Oh good, you are here," Jessica, a friend and fellow volunteer for the haunted house, greeted me in the drive as the dogs and I approached my cabin.

"I was just taking the dogs for a walk. What's up?"

"I was on my way back into town from visiting my cousin in Big Fork, and I drove by the haunted house. I'm sure I noticed a light coming from inside.

It didn't necessarily look like a light was on; it looked more like someone was moving around inside with a flashlight. I didn't have your phone number with me, but I did remember where you lived, and it was on the way so I thought I'd stop by."

"Thanks. I'm glad you did. I'll head over and check it out."

Jessica looked toward the cabin behind me. "Is Tony here?"

"He is actually out of town."

"Well, I wouldn't head over to the house alone. Who knows who you might find. It could be dangerous."

"It's probably our prankster. I'll call Mike and have him meet me over there."

She blew out a breath. "Oh good. I feel better about that." She turned and looked back toward her car. "I need to get going. I'll see you on Friday."

"See you then, and thanks again."

I continued into the cabin. I called Mike's cell, but he didn't answer, so I left a message. I figured the intruder Jessica saw was most likely the individual Tony and I suspected had been messing around with the props, so I called to the dogs, loaded them into my Jeep, and headed down the highway toward the isolated estate. When I arrived, the place looked to be closed up tight. I used my key to enter and turned on the lights. Looking toward the dogs to provide a cue if there was an intruder on the property, I waited while they sniffed around, and when they didn't seem overly concerned, I decided to take a look around. I really didn't know who our prankster was, but as Tony and I had discussed, so far the intruder had actually made things better so we'd decided not to stress over figuring it out.

I didn't see anything on the first floor and was about to head up to the second floor when I heard a crash which sounded like it had come from the basement. Changing direction, I headed down the stairs rather than up. The room was mostly empty, except for a stack of boxes in one corner and the old furnace in the very back. I felt a cold breeze and remembered the heating vent Susan had mentioned. There was a good chance what I'd heard was an animal that had accessed the vent and gotten inside. I turned on my flashlight, headed toward the back of the room, and confirmed that the screen for the vent was definitely not in place. Making a mental note to have it replaced, I headed back up the stairs. When the dogs and I arrived back on the first floor, both Tilly and Titan began to growl. Both dogs were looking toward the stairs to the second floor, so I gave them the command to find and then followed to see who or what had caused them to growl in the first place.

They passed the second floor and scrambled up the stairs to the attic. The door to the attic was closed. I opened the door and stepped inside. I stood in the middle of the room, looking around while the dogs sniffed at the wall leading to the hidden room. That was empty too. I supposed whoever had been here had gone down the back staircase as we came up the main staircase. I thought about the light Jessica had seen and wondered who'd been here. If I had to guess, it was someone who'd heard the rumor about the treasure and had come by to take a look for themselves. But who? Grange, the man who'd told

Joe about the treasure in the first place? Jack, the neighbor we suspect Joe had talked to about the treasure? Trent, the man Susan told me she'd broken into the house with when they were kids? Susan, who'd been reminded of the treasure when we'd discussed it? The other kids with Trent and Susan, who she never identified, would be adults now and possibly still living in the area?

Of course, the intruder might just have been whoever had been pranking us, and not someone looking for the treasure at all. I suspected they were long gone, so unless they left clues behind, I really had no idea how we would identify our prowler.

It was then that Tilly came trotting up with a hat in her mouth. I took the hat from Tilly and took a closer look at it. It was a baseball style hat with the name Plimpton Construction embroidered on the front. Could Grange have been the one to be here snooping around after all? He was the only one I could think of who knew about the treasure and would have a hat such as this. Of course, he could have simply left the hat when he was here doing repairs. I wished I knew exactly where Tilly had found it. Tony, Mike, Bree, and I had searched the area fairly well when we'd found the back stairway, but that didn't mean the hat couldn't have fallen behind a piece of furniture or off to the side when Grange was here, and no one had noticed it. I supposed I'd call Mike once again and let him decide.

Chapter 14

Thursday, October 24

Mike had spoken to Grange, and he'd assured Mike that he hadn't been anywhere near the house on Tuesday evening. He had been at the bowling alley with the other men who participated in his league, so Mike was inclined to believe him. The odd thing was that when Mike suggested that perhaps he'd left the hat at the house when he'd been there to do repairs, he'd informed Mike that he hadn't been wearing the hat and, in fact, never wore a hat since his hair was so thick that hats never fit right. He'd also said that the hats had been distributed as a promotion a couple of years before and there were quite a few people in town who still wore them. Too many in fact, he assured Mike, to really consider the hat to be a clue as to who may have been lurking around inside the house on Tuesday night or any other night for that matter.

Tony was coming home this afternoon. He'd called me last night to tell me that while the skeleton we'd found in the secret room could very well have belonged to Edward Vandenberg based on height, he had no way of knowing for certain that the skeleton had been Edward since he'd been a man of average height, not a man who'd been statistically tall or short. Tony decided to leave the bones behind since his friend agreed to continue his investigation, while Tony came back to White Eagle to dig around on the computer in the hope of finding a mention of when and where Edward Vandenberg might have died or perhaps where he might have been buried. Tony figured if we could find a death certificate or burial site, then we could probably eliminate him as a possible identity for the skeleton found behind the wall.

"Morning, Hattie," I greeted the owner of Hattie's Bakeshop as I began my route, which I'd started early in the hope of finishing early and having more time to spend with Tony once he got back. "Something smells wonderful."

Hattie handed Tilly a dog cookie. "I have both pumpkin spice and cinnamon apple muffins in the oven, and my apple popovers have just come out. Would you like one with a cup of coffee?"

"Normally, I would, but I'm in a bit of a rush today. Tony is coming home, and I want to get my route done early."

"Did he figure out who that skeleton belongs to?" Hattie asked. I'd spoken to her about the secret room and the skeleton we'd found during a visit the previous week.

"No. So far, they haven't found anything that would eliminate Ethel's father, Edward, as a potential identity, but they haven't found anything that would definitively prove that the skeleton belonged to the man either. Given the fact that Ethel lived in the house when the body was placed in the room, and the fact that her father seems to have simply disappeared, my money is on him as the resident of the room, but I'm not sure we'll ever be able to prove it with any certainty."

Hattie visibly shivered. "It is so disturbing to think of this young woman killing her father and then walling him in so that no one would ever find his remains."

"I don't know a lot about it, but it sounds like Edward was a cruel man who may very well have killed both his wives. Maybe Ethel acted in self-defense. Maybe her father became violent, and she fought back."

"Then why hide the body?" Hattie asked.

I shrugged. "I suppose she may have been afraid of what would happen if she told the truth. I don't think there was any sort of official law enforcement in the area before the town was incorporated. Whether or not she was faced with consequences for her actions would most likely have been up to the residents in the area, and who knows what they would have done."

Hattie turned toward the ovens and opened the one on the top. She adjusted the tray and closed it again. "I guess you do make a good point. Still, the whole thing just seems so tragic."

"I agree. It seems like the house has seen a tragic past. It really isn't surprising that a lot of folks think it is haunted."

"Any more pranks?" Hattie asked.

"No, but there was someone at the house on Tuesday. The dogs and I scared them off, and Mike had Gage do a couple of drive-bys yesterday. So far, the prankster hasn't done any real damage. I'd like to keep it that way."

Hattie rearranged her cooling trays in anticipation of taking the next batch from the oven. "Are you making a lot of money for the shelter?"

I smiled. "We are. I spoke to Brady yesterday, and he is going to go ahead with our plans to break ground for the new long-term care facility for hard to place animals in the spring. It'll be nice to provide an environment more like a home for these hard to place pets."

"The two of you are doing wonderful things for our community. I've spoken to a few of the other merchants who have all agreed to make large contributions to the cause over the next few months."

"That's wonderful. The long-term care facility is not going to be cheap. We can use all the donations we can get."

I chatted with Hattie for a few more minutes and then continued on my way. I'd ended up spending a lot more time with her than I'd planned, so if I wanted to get off early, I'd need to pick up the pace. Tilly and I had our route down pat, so when a drop and run was needed, we knew exactly what to do.

It wasn't until after lunch, which we skipped in favor of making up time, that a random comment provided a clue in Joe's murder that would throw me off my timing once again.

"Afternoon, Ernie. Where's Hap?"

Ernie Cole was Hap's part-time employee who only worked the counter when Hap was out.

"He had a doctor's appointment today, so I'm watching the counter."

I set the pile of mail on the counter. "I hope Hap is feeling okay."

Ernie nodded. "I think this is just a checkup, although it is his second appointment in the past couple of weeks." Ernie set the mail behind the counter. "Hap might not want me saying as much, so forget what I just said."

"No problem."

Ernie reached into the drawer beneath the cash drawer and pulled out a dog treat, which he handed to Tilly. "Did that paint work out okay for you?"

"Paint?"

"The black paint for the haunted house. Trent wasn't sure if a water-based or an oil-based paint would work best, but I suggested the oil."

"Trent?"

"Trent Mason. He said he was one of the volunteers out at the fundraiser. I let him charge the paint to your account. I hope that's okay."

I drew my brows together. "Uh, sure. That's fine. I really need to get going, but yes, the paint worked out fine."

Susan had said her friend, Trent, had known of a way to get into the house when they were kids. Could Trent be our prankster? Might he even have been the one to kill Joe? Susan said that Trent wanted his friends to break back into the house all those years ago and start opening up walls, but everyone had declined. She didn't know if he'd gone back, but she suspected that if he had, he hadn't found the treasure. Maybe he had never gone back then, but perhaps when he'd heard we planned to open up the house and use it for a fundraiser, he'd decided to go back for a second look before someone else found the treasure he considered to be his.

I looked up Trent Mason and found a home phone number. I called the number, but another male who I assumed was a son, brother, or roommate answered. They informed me that Trent was at a local burger joint where he worked as a short-order cook. I still needed to finish my route, but whoever answered the phone said that Trent would be at work until seven, so I decided to wait to talk to him until after I was done for the day.

By the time I made it to the burger joint, it was almost five. I headed to the counter and asked to speak to Trent. The kid I spoke to informed me that Trent was in the kitchen, but it was fine if I went in to speak to him as long as I didn't touch anything.

"Trent?" I asked just to confirm that the man I was speaking to was the right man.

"Yeah, I'm Trent. You're the lady running the haunted house."

"I am. In fact, the haunted house is the reason I'm here. I have reason to believe you are the one who painted our walls black."

The man had the decency to blush. "Yeah. That was me. How'd you find out?"

"That isn't important. What is important is the fact that you have been coming and going from the house with ease, so I have to wonder if perhaps you aren't responsible for Joe's death as well."

The man held up his hands. "I had nothing to do with that. I swear. I have been in the house a few times, but that was to look for a treasure I heard about when I was a kid. I've always wondered about the treasure, so when I heard that you were going to open up the house, I decided to look around before someone else found it. I guess I might have punched a hole in one of the walls in the downstairs while following a hunch that didn't pan out. I fixed the wall, but I didn't have the same color paint you'd used, so I used the green paint I had in my garage. I went back a second time to take another look around and decided the green was pretty hideous, so I bought the black paint and repainted all the walls downstairs. It really does look better."

"It does, but that isn't really the point." I paused as I considered what the point might be. I remembered that Mike had already gotten an alibi from Trent for the night Joe was killed. I supposed that our killer and our prankster could be two different people. "So I get why you painted the walls, but what was up with the skeleton in the bathtub?"

The guy shrugged. "I figured if all I did was paint the walls, someone might figure out why I'd painted the walls, so I did some other stuff to divert attention from the walls. I tried to make alterations that would enhance the experience. I really wasn't trying to sabotage you or the fundraiser."

"Then why did you change the locks?"

"I was afraid you'd find the open vent and secure it, so I figured if I changed the locks, I'd have a key and could continue to get back in as often as I wanted."

"Were you there on Tuesday?"

He nodded.

"Are you the one to leave a puddle of water and wet footprints in the attic?"

He looked genuinely surprised. "No. That wasn't me."

"What about the crying?"

"Crying? What crying?"

Well that was interesting. Maybe we really did have a ghost. "Have you found the treasure?"

"No. At this point, I've decided it most likely never existed. I've looked everywhere."

"Did you know about the hidden staircase and secret room before we found them?"

He flipped a burger. "Actually, no. I suspected there might be hidden passages, which is why I was punching holes in the walls, but I didn't know for certain if they existed or where they were located. I don't suppose you've found the treasure?"

"We have not," I confirmed.

"Look, I didn't mean to cause you any heartache. I guess once I got started with the pranks, they sort of got away from me. I'd offer to pay for the damage, the paint, and other supplies I charged to you, but I'm broke. This job doesn't even pay enough to cover my rent even though I have three roommates."

I wanted to be mad, but somehow I wasn't. I guess I understood how what happened might have happened, and he really did make the haunted house better. "When you were at the house, did you ever see anyone else lurking around?"

"No. It was just me. I assume you are asking if I know who killed Joe. I don't. I wish I did. I actually liked the guy. But I was bowling the night Joe died, and I didn't go to the house at all that night."

"Bowling? I remember that Grange was also bowling on the night Joe died. I assume you are in the same league?"

"We are. Different teams, but the same league. I don't remember seeing Grange there that night, but maybe he was. The bowling alley was packed, so I might have missed him."

I noticed that the man who'd been working the counter had poked his head in the door to check on the progress of the meals Trent was making.

"I should go," I said. "We are still looking for Joe's killer. If you've been in and out of the house, you might have seen something. It could even be something that didn't stand out as being relevant at the time. If you think of something, call me. I'll leave you my cell number."

"There probably aren't a lot of people who know about the secret staircase. I've spent a lot of time poking around that house, and I never found it. In my mind, if you can figure out who knew about the staircase, you'll find your killer."

"I suppose that's true unless Joe was the one who knew where the staircase was located and whoever was with him accessed the staircase and the clock tower with him."

He bobbed his head. "Yeah, I guess that's true. I didn't think to look at things from that angle."

I turned to leave.

"Listen," Trent added, "if you do find the treasure, will you tell me? I don't expect to claim it at this point, but I have always wondered. It'd be nice to get an answer to that particular question."

"If I find it, I'll let you know," I promised.

Chapter 15

By the time Tilly and I got home, Tony was waiting at my cabin. I'd missed him a lot more than I'd expected to. In a way, it bothered me that I'd become so dependent on his presence. I liked to think of myself as an independent sort who didn't need anyone to keep me company, but I guess that somewhere along the way, I'd gotten used to Tony's presence, and now I feared I not only enjoyed it but had come to need it as well.

"I'm so glad you're back," I wrapped my arms around his neck, and planted a big kiss on his lips.

"Me too. It was nice to spend some time in DC, but I missed you."

I hugged him hard one more time and then took a step back. "Any news about our skeleton since we last spoke?"

"Not really. It appears possible that the skeleton we found actually is the remains of Edward Vandenberg, but so far, we haven't found any markers that would definitely identify him as such. It does appear that the man had a poor diet based on his bone density when he died. There are many reasons for that, but poverty is the most prevalent reason. We know that Edward was a wealthy man, so that doesn't really fit. Of course, the man could simply have been a finicky eater, or he may have had dental issues he never dealt with, which led to his dietary issues. He could even have had digestive issues. It is hard to know any of this based on the remains after all this time."

"So what is the plan from this point?"

"My friend is going to run some additional tests, and I am going to get on the internet and start digging around. Maybe I can find something somewhere in one type of historical document or another that will provide us with information we don't currently have. At the very least, if he did return to England, maybe I can find proof of that. If nothing else, it would eliminate the possibility that he had ended up in the sealed secret room." Tony bent down to pick up Tinder who was trying to crawl up his leg. "So how are things here?"

"I found out who our prankster is." I filled Tony in on my conversation with Trent.

"I guess all that makes sense," Tony said after I'd shared the details of why Trent had broken in, and why he'd put his own touch on the decorations.

"I'm not happy he did what he did without informing us as to what he was doing, but I don't suppose any real harm has been done. At least we shouldn't have to worry about any more late-night visits."

"Do you know if Mike has made any progress on Joe's murder?" Tony asked.

"Not as of the last time I spoke to him. I know he has interviewed a lot of people, but so far, everyone he has talked to has an alibi for the night Joe died."

"What if the timeline Mike has been working from is off?" Tony asked.

"What do you mean?"

"According to Joe's wife, he was at the house doing the volunteer thing, he came home and had dinner with her, she went to bed early while he was still watching television, and he was missing by the time she awoke the following morning. I seem to remember the wife saying something about going to bed at around nine. If Mike has been operating under the assumption that Joe returned to the house right away, then he would have been looking for the location of his suspects at around that time. But what if Joe didn't go back to the house right away? An alibi such as the fact that Grange was bowling would work if the murder occurred at nine or maybe even ten, but what if the murder occurred at two or three a.m.?"

"So you think Grange did it?"

"Not necessarily," Tony corrected. "I was just using Grange as an example. Mike said that Joe most likely died at some point between the time his wife went to bed and daylight. There are a lot of hours between those two points. The alibis Mike has been gathering only work if Joe was killed shortly after his wife retired for the evening. If he was killed later that night, then none of the alibis Mike has gathered really work. Or at least none of the alibis I know of."

"I think Jack was out of town, so his alibi probably stands, but I do remember that Grange's alibi was bowling as was Trent's. Both would have been done by eleven. Maybe even sooner."

Tony nodded. "Exactly. I've given this some thought, and I think that Mike needs to establish a timeline for each suspect that includes the overnight hours. Unless, of course, he has already done so, but just hasn't mentioned it, which I assume is a possibility."

"I'll call and ask him. In fact, unless you are too tired, I'll see if Mike and Bree want to come over. We can order a pizza and go over everything one more time."

"Sounds good to me. I need to make a few calls, but I should be done in twenty minutes or so."

A quick call to Mike netted me with the information that he and Bree had not eaten yet and that they'd like to get together. He suggested we go over to their place since Bree had made lasagna, which only needed heating, and we agreed. Tony grabbed a couple of bottles of wine while I changed out of my uniform. Tilly had been walking all day, and Tony had walked Titan when he'd gotten home, so we fed all the animals and headed out.

Mike and Bree currently lived in the house which had belonged to Bree for quite some time before they even started dating. There had been talk about them looking for a house that was "theirs" rather than "hers," but so far, they hadn't gotten around to it. Bree had a nice home in a pleasant part of town, but I knew she still considered the place "hers." She'd make comments about Mike messing up *her* kitchen or leaving his socks on the floor of *her* bedroom. In my opinion, a home that represented neutral ground might be a good idea. Of course, Bree's home was close to both her bookstore and Mike's office, and it was on a quiet street, so in terms of location, it was going to be hard to beat.

The first thing I noticed when arriving at Mike and Bree's was the smell of garlic. I'd always loved Italian food, but since I began dating Tony and he started cooking for me, I'd come to appreciate really good Italian food in a way I never had before.

"It smells wonderful in here," I said to Bree, who was working in the kitchen when we arrived.

"I made two casseroles the last time I made lasagna and froze one, so we could just heat it up on a weekday. It's warming in the oven, and I have garlic bread under the broiler." Bree glanced at the wine in my hand. "I see you brought some of Tony's stash."

I nodded and then crossed the room to the drawer where I knew Bree kept her corkscrew. "Tony has started leaving some of his good wine at my place for those occasions when we stay at the cabin. I was never a wine snob before, but now that I've had really good wine that I could never afford on my own, I find that I have become a bit more discriminate. Which glasses do you want me to use?"

Bree grabbed four glasses out of a cupboard and set them on the counter. I poured wine into all four glasses, and then set them on the table next to the water glasses someone had already filled.

"This is basically ready," Bree said as she slid the garlic bread from the broiler. "I have a salad in the refrigerator if you want to grab that. I'll cut the lasagna while you grab the guys."

By some sort of unvoiced agreement, we all seemed to understand that talk of murder and long-hidden bodies would wait until after we'd consumed the wonderful food Bree had made. During the meal, we discussed the upcoming harvest events in town as well as the Christmas events such as Christmas on Main which were really just around the corner. Bree hadn't heard that the committee had planned to add a carnival to the long weekend, and she had some input on the idea which we ended up discussing at length. Once the meal was over, Tony cleared the table and started the dishes, while Bree and I put the leftover food away. When Mike grabbed a beer and headed toward the living room, I gave him the evil eye which had him offering to help Tony, while Bree and I relaxed. It didn't take long to get the kitchen in order, so by the time Bree and I had opened the second bottle of wine, Tony and Mike joined us near the white brick fireplace.

"So what did you learn in DC?" Mike asked after we'd all gotten settled.

Tony filled him in. We didn't really know a lot, but we did know that the skeleton at least had the potential to have belonged to Edward Vandenberg, but even Mike expressed his doubt when Tony informed him that the person whose body had been left in the sealed secret room had suffered from nutritional deficiencies in life. As Tony and I had discussed, it was possible the man had health issues or simply bad eating habits that led to the deficiencies, but the more likely explanation was poverty.

Once we'd exhausted the discussion of the skeleton in the secret room, Tony brought up Joe's death. He started off by asking Mike about the time limitations of the alibis.

"A lot of the alibis are indeed based on the premise that Joe headed back to the house shortly after his wife went to bed," Mike said. "I guess it just made sense that the guy would head out as soon as he was able, but I may need to rethink things. There is still the problem of finding anyone who had both motive and opportunity. I can come up with a list of people who had a beef with the guy who could not have physically gotten up into the clock tower and killed the man, and I have a list of folks who we know knew about the clock tower and had the physical ability to access it but don't seem to have a motive, but I'm short on folks who fall into both categories."

"It does seem that the number of people who even had the potential to know that Joe had gone back to the house that night is limited," Bree said.

"What if he was followed?" I asked.

Mike frowned. "Followed? Followed how?"

"What if someone had been watching his house and when Joe left, his killer followed him."

"Why would someone be watching Joe's house?" Mike asked. "Even if someone had a beef with Joe, it makes no sense the killer would just be sitting there looking for an opportunity to act."

I supposed Mike was right. The idea that someone would be sitting outside the man's house waiting for him to leave was pretty thin.

"What about the wife?" I asked.

Mike raised a brow, but he did give me his attention.

"The wife was the one to report him missing," I pointed out. "She said he was watching television when she went to bed and that when she awoke, he was gone, but do you know this for certain? The couple didn't have children and lived alone. Isn't it possible that she followed him to the house?"

"Why would she do that?" Mike asked. "If she wanted to kill the guy, she could have just put cyanide in his meatloaf."

"What if she didn't mean to kill him? What if she saw him leave and followed him. Maybe she suspected an affair and wanted to see where he was going. Once they got to the house, she followed him into the secret passage, and something happened. I don't know what exactly, but maybe he ended up dead, and the wife panicked and fled. After she got home, she made up the story about going to bed early."

"Seems unlikely," Mike said.

"Maybe," I agreed. "But what about Grange?"

"What about Grange?" Mike asked me.

"You said that Grange and Joe had discussed the treasure, and you said that Grange's alibi was bowling. Grange has made it sound as if he was fine with the fact that his friend and employee went into competition with him, but what if he really wasn't as fine as he is trying to make out?" I asked, continuing my line of questioning. "I like Grange. We've known each other for a long time, and I want to believe he wouldn't kill anyone, but he really does make a good suspect. Even Grange said that if Joe was going to go after the treasure, it made sense that he would be the person Joe would call for help. Maybe Joe did just that, the two men met up at the house, there was a struggle of some sort, and Joe died. Other than Joe, and possibly Trent, Grange is the person most likely to have known about the secret passage, and he has the physical ability to both kill Joe and to leave him in the clock tower."

"He does have a motive," Bree said.

"And even if he was at the bowling alley, he could have gone over to the house when he finished for the night," Tony said.

"And we found a hat inside the house that he said was not his, but totally could be since it is from his company," I added.

"We could test the hat for DNA," Mike said. "That won't prove that the person wearing the hat killed Joe, but if Grange is lying about the hat being his, testing it for DNA could at least prove that much. I'll take a look and see what I can find tomorrow."

"In the meantime, we have the second weekend of the haunted house to get through," I reminded everyone. "I guess we should refocus at least some of our attention on that."

Chapter 16

Friday, October 25

By the next afternoon, Mike was convinced our theory that Grange was the killer might have merit. None of us wanted to believe it, but after we'd made the points we had the previous evening, Mike began to dig deeper.

"After we spoke," Mike said to me after I'd stopped by with his mail, "I pulled the financial records for both Grange Plimpton and Plimpton Construction. Personally, it seems as if Grange is doing okay. He seems to have managed his money well over the years, and I didn't find any red flags. The company, however, seems to be struggling. In fact, I would go as far as to say that in the past few months, they've ventured into a fairly serious financial situation which seems to be further exasperated by the fact that Grange's brother, Greg, is going through a messy divorce and struggling with his own financial issues. It seems that Greg had been putting pressure on Grange to do something about the fact that Joe has been stealing their business."

"So the business is struggling because Joe left?" I asked.

"It's hard to say specifically what caused the decline in income, but it does look as if Joe took some of Plimpton Construction's customers with him."

I slid my bag off my shoulder and set it on the floor. Mike and I were talking in his office, and I'd left Tilly out in the reception area with Frank and Leonard. "Grange told me that he held no ill will toward Joe for wanting to do his own thing. At the time, I felt he was being sincere, but if his leaving affected the company's bottom line in a negative way, that might cause me to take a second look at things."

"I know seeing the financial records caused me to take a second look at things," Mike said. "If you remember, we initially suspected that Joe might have called someone and asked them to meet him at the house."

"I remember."

"I never found proof of this, so we entertained other theories. It seems as if Joe did send a text that night, but since he didn't send it from his phone, I didn't find it in his phone records."

"If he didn't use his cell, how did he send the text?"

"He used his wife's phone. I just found this out this morning after she finally decided to return the dozen or so messages I'd left for her while she was at her sister's. She said she hadn't initially realized that Joe had used her phone that night, and even when she saw the text, she didn't think much of it. She remembered Joe complaining that his phone was dead and he needed to charge it, but he'd left it in his truck and didn't feel like going out to get it. She remembered that she'd left her phone right there on the coffee table, so she figured he just used it since it was convenient."

"Who did Joe text?" I asked.

"Grange Plimpton."

I audibly gasped. "Really?"

Mike nodded. "The text said that he was going to go back to the haunted house to take a look around. It also said that when he was there that day, he'd noticed something he hadn't noticed before and wanted to check out. As we suspected, he told Grange he'd left one of the windows in the hallway unlatched."

"So what did Grange say when you told him that?"

"He said he never received any such text. He even showed me his phone, and the text and his response were not there."

"So he must have deleted them."

"That is my theory, although Grange swears that he didn't delete the text and that he never saw the text. I showed him the response sent to Joe's wife's phone from his, which said that he would meet him at the house, but he swears he has no idea how it got there."

"He's lying."

"Maybe. But it didn't seem like he was lying."

I blew out a breath. "Okay. So Joe texted Grange, and Grange responded that he would meet him at the house. I assume that Grange is still maintaining that he wasn't at the house that evening."

"He is. He said that he went directly to the bowling alley after work. He was there until about eleven, and then he went home. He admitted that it made perfect sense that Joe would have texted him if he planned to go back to the house that night, and if he'd gotten the text, he probably would have met him there when his bowling league let out, but he also swears that is not what happened. It is possible that someone else saw the text, responded, and then erased the text. Grange did say he leaves his phone in his truck a lot of the time, and that a lot of people know about his habit. He also said that he might have left it right there on the table when he was bowling. He admitted he's been known to do that as well."

"He wasn't sure which?"

Mike shook his head. "He said he didn't really remember."

"So if he did leave it lying around somewhere and someone did see the text and respond, they could have deleted the text from his phone, and he might never have known."

"Theoretically yes."

I paused to think about it. "I guess it could have happened that way."

"I guess," Mike agreed. "But it sort of seems unlikely. Still, all I have at this point are a lot of facts that don't amount to a smoking gun. I'll need more for an arrest."

"I suppose that even if you could prove that Grange had received the text and responded, that still wouldn't prove that he'd met up with Joe on the night he died and it certainly wouldn't prove he'd killed him."

"Exactly."

"So, what now?" I asked.

"I guess I'll keep digging. I really hate to think Grange is our killer, but he does seem to have had a motive if Joe leaving and taking clients has affected his company's bottom line, and it appears that he knew Joe was going to be at the house, giving him the opportunity to meet him there, and take care of his problem. Additionally, he is a big strong guy, so unlike some of the others with a motive, he seems to have the means to carry out the murder as well. At this point, the only person possessing the perfect trifecta of motive, means, and opportunity is Grange. I hope it's not him, but it is beginning to look that way.

Chapter 17

After Tilly and I left Mike's office, we continued on our route. It was Friday, which meant I had two days off. Sure, I had to be at the haunted house every afternoon and evening, but I would also be able to sleep in a bit, and enjoy breakfast with Tony and the animals over the weekend. In the past, Tony and I had made our own Halloween plans which always included a spooky movie marathon, but with the fundraiser this year, it looked as if a Halloween Spookathon would have to wait. We could stay up late and watch scary movies on Wednesday night, but I did have to work on Thursday, and Thursday would be a late night being that it was Halloween and the final night of the haunted house, so perhaps that wouldn't work. Unless…

I took out my phone and called my supervisor. "Hey, Margie, it's Tess. I know this is late notice, but I was wondering if there was any way I could take Thursday and Friday off next week. We have the fundraiser on Thursday, and I'll have clean up the weekend after that. I have a bunch of vacation days saved up, so that won't be a problem."

"I'll see if I can get coverage. We have some new temps that have been asking for hours, so I don't anticipate a problem. If I can get a carrier lined up, I should be able to process the last minute request. You'll still need to do the paperwork to turn into the main office."

"I'll do it when I come in this evening. And thanks. If you can find someone to cover for me, I'll owe you."

"I do like it when my carriers owe me," Margie chuckled.

Okay, suddenly things were looking up. I had the haunted house tonight, Saturday, and Sunday night, and I'd have work Monday through Wednesday, but then Tony and I could do the spooky movie thing on Wednesday night if I didn't have work on Thursday, and if I had Friday off, we could get a head start on the cleanup so we wouldn't need to devote the entire weekend to tearing down the props that had taken an entire crew a weekend to set up. The haunted house had certainly been a lot more work than a pet parade would have been, but when we opened the residence for hard to place pets, I knew that all the work would seem worth it.

The last stop on my route today was an antique store owned by a woman named Star Moonwalker. When I'd first met her, I assumed the name was an alias, but it was the name she went by, and it was the name on the certified letter I'd been tasked with delivering. Normally, Star received her mail via a mailbox at the main post office, but it was Friday, and the letter required a signature, so instead of just sticking the letter behind the counter and holding it until Star could come in next week and sign for it, I'd been asked to deliver it and obtain the signature while I was at it.

"Thank you so much for bringing this by." Star signed for the letter and then held it in both her hands almost reverently. As you would expect from someone named Star Moonwalker, she had a natural presence, calm manner, and casual style, reminiscent of the flower child look of the sixties.

"It must be important," I commented.

"It might be." She paused, looked around, and then leaned in a bit as if to share a confidence. "Not a lot of people know this, but I was adopted, and about four years ago, I decided to look for my birth parents. It's been a rocky road, and things have not turned out the way I hoped, but I still feel committed to seeing this through at this point, and this envelope might contain the information I've been waiting for."

I turned to leave, but she continued. It seemed as if she wanted to talk about whatever was on her mind, so I waited.

"My adoptive parents hadn't wanted me to look for my birth parents. I guess in retrospect, they were right to feel that way." She let out a noise that sounded like a snort. "If I knew then what I know now, I would have listened to them, but at the time, I was curious, and you know the saying that curiosity killing the cat."

I had to wonder where Star was going with this and was about to respond, but she continued.

"My adoptive mom passed away eight years ago, and my adoptive dad followed three years later. I spent a year struggling with the voice in the back of my mind telling me that now was the time to look for my birth parents before I finally did decide to take the plunge and start the process. I knew it wouldn't be easy since I'd been left at a church as an infant and didn't even have a birth certificate, but I still wanted to try."

"And?"

"Three years ago, I hired a man named Sam Denton to find my parents. It took him about a year to track down the nun I'd been surrendered to since I'd actually provided him very little information to work with. The nun told Denton that the man who'd dropped me off had told her that the baby's mother had died and the baby needed a home. The nun tried to get additional information about the baby and the baby's parents from the man, but he refused to answer. Once the baby was safely in the nun's arms, he left. The nun thought the whole thing was odd, but she wanted me to have a safe and happy home, so she found a wonderful couple to adopt me named Sonny and Dharma Moonwalker."

"So did you ever get the rest of the story?" I wondered.

She nodded. "Part of it. Denton did some digging, and eventually found out that on the same date I was dropped off at the church in Great Falls, Montana, a woman was found shot to death in Buffalo, Wyoming. It was noted in the police report filed after her death that the victim had recently given birth. The detective in charge of the case looked for the baby in Wyoming, but he or she was never found. I'm not sure why no one put two and two together at the time, I guess the fact that the man who dropped me at the church crossed state lines might have had something to do with it. It wasn't until Denton started poking around that it was determined that I was most likely the baby the woman had delivered before she died."

"Wow. That's really sad."

Star bowed her head. "It is sad. In fact, once I found out that my mother had been shot and killed shortly after delivering me, I pretty much decided to give up the idea of searching for answers to my past. I thanked Denton for what he'd done, paid him what I owed him, and asked him not to look for my father. I decided to make peace with the fact that I'd been raised by wonderful people who'd never treated me any less than a real daughter and get on with my life."

I leaned a hip against a counter. "I'm sensing the story doesn't end there."

"It doesn't. Denton did drop it when I asked him to, but a couple of years later, another case for another client brought him back into my life."

"How?" I asked, being pulled into the story almost against my will.

"It seems that Denton had been hired to find proof that a man who had been living under an alias for years and everyone believed dead was actually alive."

My breath caught in my throat. This was beginning to sound much too familiar.

"During the course of backtracking to figure out what had really happened to the guy, Denton came across the report filed by the detective who'd been assigned to investigate the murder of the woman who'd been shot in Buffalo on the day I was dropped off at the church in Great Falls. Denton realized immediately that the woman mentioned in the report was the same women he believed had actually been my mother."

"Was there new information in the report?" I asked, almost afraid to breathe.

"There was. It turns out there was a copy of an interview conducted by the detective who investigated at the time of the shooting with the owner of the apartment building his victim had lived in during the final months of her pregnancy."

"And?"

"The apartment owner was able to provide the detective with the names of the couple who'd rented the apartment. Or at least the names they'd given her. She also had a copy of the driver's license provided by the man who accompanied the woman. It was the impression of the woman who owned the apartment building that the man accompanying the pregnant woman had been the father of the baby, although she did admit to the detective that neither the man nor woman had said as much."

"So the man Denton had been hired to find was the same man who'd been traveling with the woman believed to be your mother?"

"Yes. It looked that way. Denton managed to obtain a copy of the rental agreement from the woman who owned the apartment building since apparently, she has kept every rental agreement she'd ever issued. Anyway, as I mentioned, the agreement on file included a copy of the driver's license provided by the man who had been with the murder victim. Denton checked it out and found out that the license was a fake and the name on the license had been an alias, but the license did provide a photo of the man, so on a hunch, Denton made a copy of the license and showed the photo to the nun I'd been surrendered to. She verified that the man who'd dropped me off at the church almost forty years earlier was the same man in the photo."

"So the man who dropped you at the church was probably your father?"

"Probably. That is what Denton believed, although there was really no way to know for sure if the man was my father or if he was just traveling with the woman I believed to be my mother for some reason. After a bit of soul searching, I decided that it was likely I'd never know the answer to that question, so once again, I decided to drop it."

I looked at the letter in the woman's hands. "I'm sensing that wasn't the end of it."

She shook her head. "As it turns out, even though I was no longer paying him to look for my father, Denton's other client was still paying him to find the truck driver everyone other than Denton's client seemed to believe was dead. And since the man Denton had been hired to find appeared to have been the same man who dropped me at the church, Denton was actually still looking for my father in a parallel sort of way. This past spring, Denton wrote and told me that he'd managed to track down the man he'd been looking for, and had in fact been able to provide photos of the man to the client who'd hired him."

My hand flew to my throat. I really wish I could stop her here, but I also knew I needed to hear the rest. I supposed Star hadn't noticed my reaction since she continued.

"As it turned out, while Denton had been hired to find the guy and offer proof of life, he hadn't been asked to do anything beyond that, so in terms of the client Denton had been working for up to that point, once he had the photos proving the man actually was alive, he was finished. He did, however, have my situation in the back of his mind, so he offered to continue to track the man."

"And?" I croaked, barely louder than a whisper.

"And, I told him I needed a couple of days to think things over. He agreed to continue to follow the guy while I made up my mind. I'd all but decided to let the whole thing go when I found out that Denton had been shot and killed. I'm pretty sure the man who may or may not be my father killed him." She looked at the envelope. "This is a copy of the file Denton built on the man before his death. He'd given it to a friend for safekeeping. The friend knew about my situation and agreed to send it to me."

Oh god. I held my breath as she ripped open the envelope and pulled out a stack of papers. On the top was a copy of the driver's license provided to the woman who owned the apartment building by the man who was accompanying the pregnant woman who'd been shot and killed shortly after giving birth. The photo on the license was that of a young Grant Thomas. The name on the license, however, was Grant Tucker.

Chapter 18

Holy sh… Did this woman just tell me that her father and my father were the same person? Did she also just tell me that she thought our father killed the man she'd hired to find him? I felt like I should say something, anything, but my mind refused to form a coherent sentence, so I simply mumbled something about giving her some privacy, turned, and walked away.

The only good thing about learning what I'd learned when and how I'd learned it was that Star Moonwalker's certified letter was my last stop of the day. I almost run back to my Jeep, loaded Tilly inside, and then headed to the post office to drop off my now empty bag. Margie informed me that she'd received approval for my days off next week. I'm pretty sure I responded. I just hope my response was in the form of a thank you. I headed home to change my clothes and try to get a grip on my emotions. Tony had already left for the haunted house, which I knew he planned to do, but that was okay. I really did need a minute to pull myself together.

Now that I'd had a moment to think, I really did have so many questions, including the question of how and when this had happened. Star said something about all this occurring forty years ago. That would mean she was left at the church before my dad even met and started dating my mom. I supposed that made me feel somewhat better than I would have felt if Star had been the product of an affair between my dad and this other woman. But Star also indicated that she thought the man who'd dropped her at the church had killed the PI she'd paid to track the man down. Was that true? Had my father actually killed Denton in order to keep his secret? And if he had killed Denton, was Star in danger as well?

I looked at Tilly. "This can't be real. I'm dreaming. Right?"

"Ruff," she barked.

There really had to be another explanation. Yes, it did appear on the surface that my father and Star's father were one and the same, and I had no reason to believe she'd lied about the fact that the man Denton had tracked down may have ended up killing him, but maybe she was simply wrong. I knew that my dad had a lot of people after him. Maybe Denton was being tracked by whoever had been tracking Dad, in addition to Tony and I of course, and it was these men, the men who'd tried to convince us they were CIA, who had killed the PI who'd discovered more than he should have.

"Okay, Tess this is not the time to lose it," I said aloud as I gathered my stuff for the evening. "I'm sure there is a rational explanation for all of this. I don't know what this explanation is offhand, but I know there must be one." I took several deep breaths. "Right now, you have a haunted house to get to. It's important that you are there. People are counting on you. When it's over, you can talk to Tony about this. He'll know what to do. Tony always knows what to do."

I forced my legs to climb the stairs, where I changed into jeans and a sweatshirt. I pulled on tennis shoes, called to Titan, and took both dogs for a quick walk since I wasn't sure how long Tony had been at the haunted house. Once both dogs had done their business, I fed all the animals, and then as calmly as I could, I drove to the haunted house. How on earth was I going to get through this night without blabbing everything I knew to Mike and Bree? "Just breathe," I said aloud. I tried to do just that but ended up coughing rather than breathing.

"Are you okay?" Bree asked, after approaching my Jeep from the side. She must have seen me drive up and had come over to greet me.

"I'm fine. I just swallowed wrong. How is everything going so far?"

Bree answered. "Things are going fine. There is a tiny problem with the electrical breaker on the first floor, but Tony is fixing it. I'm sure it will be fine." She looked at me more intently. "Are you sure you are feeling okay? You look sort of off."

"I'm fine. It's just been a long day. But it is the weekend now, and I managed to get two days off at the end of next week, so I'm all good. Let's go and see if Tony needs any help."

Fortunately, the night went off without a hitch. We had even more visitors than we'd had last weekend, but with the extra tours, we'd been able to accommodate everyone. The ticket sales were being deposited directly into an account Brady had set up for the expansion, so I didn't have an actual number to assign to the ticket sales, but I was pretty sure that we'd made a lot more than our original projections called for. Brady had worked the ticket desk this evening, and every time I checked in with him, he had a group of locals who were asking about what they could do to help with the project.

Once the haunted house was closed for the day, Tony and I, along with a group of volunteers, cleaned up and locked up before we all went our separate ways.

"I have news." Tony and I said aloud at exactly the same time after we arrived back at the cabin.

"Go ahead," Tony offered.

"No. Mine is complicated. You go first," I countered.

"Okay," Tony agreed. "My buddy from DC called today. He's had a little more time to look at the skeleton, and he told me he found a nick on one of the ribs on the left side of the body which he believes resulted from a stab wound to the chest. Most likely, the stab wound that killed our skeleton."

"I guess I was half expecting that the guy died from a stab wound. I'm not sure why. Anything else?"

"He believes the victim in the secret room was a young man who was probably in his twenties when he died."

I raised a brow. "That eliminates Edward Vandenberg as the victim."

"It does. After taking a closer look at things, it seems likely that someone other than Edward was in the sealed secret room."

"Okay, who? As far as I know, Ethel was an only child. Her mother would have been dead by the time the skeleton was encased in the secret room, so it stands to reason that Ethel or her father put the guy there." I paused to consider this. "I know we've speculated as to the date the room was added to the house, but is there a way to really narrow this down? It seems if we are going to figure out who was in the room, we need to figure out when he was put there."

"The coroner mentioned that the body could have been in the sealed secret room as early as the thirties, but I did some research and found out that the type of drywall used to construct the room wasn't widely available until World War II. So I'm going to go out on a limb and say the skeleton we found in the room has only been there since the mid- to late-nineteen-forties. Ethel would have been in her thirties by this point, so it seems to me that either Ethel or her father could have been responsible for the man's murder."

I let the dogs out and then stood with Tony on the porch and waited for them to do their thing. "We have unconfirmed intel that Ethel had been living alone in the house for a good part of her adult life, although we should keep in mind that while a lot of people have been tossing around a lot of general comments, no one seems to know with any degree of certainty exactly what happened or exactly when it happened. Do we know anything else about the skeleton that could point us to an identity?" I asked. "Other than the fact he was probably in his twenties when he died, was of average height, most likely died of a stab wound to the chest, and seemed to have consumed a less than adequate diet."

"My friend from DC did say that the skeleton showed signs of damage to his back, even though the victim was young. He suspected that he engaged in an activity that required a lot of bending and lifting."

"Like working for a lumber mill."

Tony nodded. "That would fit the bill. I found out that Edward Vandenberg only worked in the lumber industry for a short time. He opened his small mill in the twenties, but by the time the Westons and the Wades took over the lumber industry in the early forties, he'd shut down operations. If our victim was murdered in the forties or later as we now suspect, then he would have been working for Weston and Wade rather than Vandenberg when he died."

"If this guy was some random lumber worker, the odds of us ever identifying him are slim to none," I said.

"I agree. Unless we can find something, a news article perhaps, that mentions a young male living at the Vandenberg house who later went missing. Perhaps a groundskeeper or a stable hand." Tony looked at me. "So you said you had news?"

I blew out a breath. "Yeah. Mine is pretty heavy, so maybe we should pour ourselves a glass of wine first."

Tony looked uncertain. "Okay. A glass of wine sounds nice. Would you like me to build a fire while you pour the wine?"

I hesitated. "Actually, I think we are going to need the computers at your place. Maybe we should pack everyone up and head in that direction. I'll fill you in on the way."

"Is everything okay?"

"Honestly, I'm really not sure."

I really hadn't meant to freak Tony out, and then make him wait for an explanation, but that is exactly what I'd ended up doing. He never said a word after I began to recant my conversation with Star, but I could see that his mind was working a million miles a minute. By the time I'd gotten to the part where Denton had died, most likely as a result of his search for the man I was convinced was my father, Tony's smile had turned into a deep scowling frown.

"Do you really think your father killed this man?" Tony asked.

"I don't know. I hope not, but maybe. If there is one thing that I've learned over the past two years, it is that the man I thought was my father never really existed."

I sort of thought that Tony would make a comment about knowing the man beneath the exterior in my heart, but he didn't. I guess he had the same doubts I did.

"What should we do?" I asked after a moment.

"What do you want to do?"

I leaned my head back against the headrest and closed my eyes. God, I was tired. "I don't know. If my dad is a killer, I don't want to know the truth, but there is a part of me that needs to know. It occurred to me that we should track him down and ask him. Not that he is an easy man to track down, but we have gotten close to him in the past. I have no reason to think we couldn't again. Of course, he did ask us to stop looking for him. He did say that not only did our search put him in danger, but it also put Mom, Mike, and me in danger as well. I remember the guys who showed up at your house, and I remember the men who pulled Mike aside at dinner. I'm sure Dad was not exaggerating about the danger," I blew out a breath, "but does that mean I do nothing? Does that mean I find out that not only might I have a sister but also that she might be putting herself in danger by looking for the same man you and I had been tracking before we decided it was too dangerous to continue?"

"How well do you know Star?" Tony asked.

"Not well at all. Certainly not well enough to simply pull her aside and warn her to back off."

Tony slowly pulled onto the drive leading to his house. In spite of the angst I was bogged down in, I smiled when I noticed the orange lights he'd hung in the trees. I knew he'd hung them for me after I'd admired the ones in town.

"I guess we could start by looking into Star's background," Tony suggested. "It seems it might be a good idea to check out the story she told you. It could be that the story provided by her PI was less than factual, and even if it is based in fact, it is possible that some of the facts could have been made up or exaggerated. If it turns out that the PI did provide her with good intel, and it really does look as if this woman is your sister, then we can decide to dig deeper. There is no reason to disturb the hornet's nest until we know for certain what we are dealing with."

"Okay," I said as Tony pulled the truck to a stop. "That's a good idea. We'll start with Star, and then see where we end up."

Once we unloaded the animals, I set about getting them settled while Tony started a fire. His command center was located in his basement, which was functional but lacking in warmth or personality. He figured he could start our search on his laptop, which he brought to the table near the fireplace, and then if we needed more computing power at some point, we could move downstairs.

I poured us each a glass of wine while Tony logged onto his computer. I knew from experience that the only way I could help was by sitting quietly and waiting for him to do what he needed to do. After a few minutes, he began to speak.

"Star Moonwalker was adopted by Sonny and Dharma Moonwalker in nineteen seventy-nine."

"So before Mom and Dad married and a year before Grant Thomas first showed up."

"Correct. Star told you that the man she believed to be her father had a driver's license with the name Grant Tucker. After Star's mother was shot, he must have given up the name Grant Tucker and taken on the name Grant Thomas, which is the name he was using when he met your mother."

"We know that the gang at the lake he visited every year around Thanksgiving called my dad Tuck." I rubbed my hands up and down my arms, which had suddenly become covered in goosebumps. "I guess he'd been going to the lake while he'd been using the name Tucker."

"It looks that way."

I leaned back and groaned. "Who was this man?"

Tony reached out and grasped my hand. "Do you want to continue?"

I nodded.

Tony returned to his keyboard. "I'm looking at the history of Star's parents. It looks as if her adoptive mother was born as Sarah Rutherford and her adoptive father was born as Link Denmore. They met while attending college at UC Berkeley, and both seemed to embrace the hippie revival movement. When they married, they legally changed their names to Sonny and Dharma Moonwalker. After college, they moved first to Denver and then to Missoula. They adopted Star in nineteen seventy-nine and gave her their new last name, Moonwalker."

"I always thought her name was an alias, but apparently, I was wrong about that. What else does it say?"

"It appears the family moved to Sand Point, Idaho for a while and then back to Montana just before the mom getting sick. She died eight years ago from complications due to cancer. Sonny was killed in an auto accident five years ago. Star moved to White Eagle and opened her antique store three years ago."

"She told me she hired Denton four years ago. He found a trail leading to the church where Star was abandoned shortly after. The rest of what she's learned came to her over time."

Tony sat back in his chair. He paused and then began to speak. "So it looks like that at some point in the late seventies, Grant Tucker moved to Wyoming and met Star's mother. Or perhaps he already knew the woman who was shot, and they came to Wyoming together. At this point, we don't know if they were legally wed, but it does look as if the woman with Grant was pregnant, and I would suspect that either Grant was the father of the baby, or someone else was the father and Grant was helping the woman for some reason. They rented an apartment in Buffalo, Wyoming where Star's mother gave birth to her. Shortly after she gave birth, she was shot and killed, and at some point, Grant took the baby to a church in

Great Falls, Montana. He left her with a nun with instructions to find the baby a good home. Sonny and Dharma were living in Kalispell at this point. I guess they must have moved from Missoula. Anyway, based on what we've found, they were chosen as Star's adoptive parents. I'm still sort of unclear on this, but it does appear, based on what you've said, that Star grew up in a happy family situation. After her adoptive parents both died, she decided to look for her birth parents and hired a PI named Sam Denton."

"That all sounds right to me."

"Meanwhile, at some point, after he dropped the baby off at the church, Grant Tucker disappeared and reemerged as Grant Thomas. He met your mother, they married, and first Mike and then you were born. Twelve years after the birth of his youngest child, he faked his own death and disappeared. We still have a lot of blanks to fill in to get us from that point until now, but we do know that he is still alive, still on the run, and assumedly using yet another name. Somehow, this PI managed to put things together, and he ended up dead. Star suspects it was Grant Tucker who killed him."

I got up and began pacing around the room. "Star told me that she told Denton not to look for her father after she found out about her mother's death. She said she thanked him, paid him off, and sent him on his way. But then someone else hired the same PI to find proof that a man who had been living under an alias for years and everyone believed to be dead was actually alive. That man turned out to be Grant Thomas, and in my mind, that somehow put Denton in a position where he needed to be eliminated. I have to wonder who it was that hired Denton to find my dad in the first place."

"I don't know," Tony turned back to his screen. "I'll see if I can find out, but it isn't going to be easy. No one who would hire a PI to find a dead man is going to be the typical PI customer. In fact, given the fact that Denton was hired for such a task, indicates to me that there is more going on than we suspect."

"I guess at this point find out what you can about Sam Denton. Somewhere in the middle of all these confusing yet surprisingly interconnected facts, lies the truth about what really happened and who is responsible for killing him." I grabbed an apple from the bowl and then sat back down. "Do you think Star is in danger?"

"Maybe," Tony answered. "She did just receive a file that has information about your father that he might not want someone having."

"Should we warn her?"

Tony paused and looked at me. "I'm not sure. Part of me thinks that telling her everything that is going on will only make her more of a target, and part of me feels that she is already a target and someone should warn her to get out of town." Tony drummed his fingers on the table. "Did it seem as if she was planning to continue to look for her father?"

"No, I don't think so. She thinks her father killed her PI. I got the impression that she is sorry she ever looked for the man in the first place and really has no interest in meeting him. It sounded like the file was sent to her based on Denton's instructions before he died. Still, once she really lets everything sink in, who knows?"

"I guess we should find out what we can, and then keep an eye on the situation." Tony turned back to his screen. "Should we tell Mike?"

"No, at least not yet. Mike is the sort who will definitely not leave it alone if he thinks our father is a killer. If he knows, he will probably just make things worse."

Chapter 19

Saturday, October 26

Tony and I had worked late into the night trying to learn what we could about Star Moonwalker, her adoptive parents, the woman who had given birth to her, the man who dropped her off at the church, and the nun who took custody of the baby in the first place. To be honest, it totally blew my mind that this man who'd been going by the name Grant Tucker, would go into hiding with the mother of his child only to witness her death and then, after abandoning their child, would turn around, change his name, marry my mom, and then have Mike and me. Wouldn't a man who had lost the mother of his child after she'd been shot, presumably by someone who was actually after him, go into deep hiding rather than moving a few hundred miles north and establishing another family less than two years later? The whole thing made no sense.

"I need to meet with Austin Wade," Tony informed me shortly after we'd finished breakfast. "I meant to mention it last night, but then you told me about Star, and I got distracted."

"Why are you meeting with Austin?" Austin Wade was the patriarch of one of the richest families in town. His grandfather, Dillinger Wade, had established the town along with his business partner, Hank Weston, in nineteen forty-five.

"After I realized that the skeleton whose identity we have been trying to establish most likely lived and worked in White Eagle during the forties, I called Austin to see if he had copies of the old local paper that used to be published monthly back in the forties. He said he did have copies, so I asked if I could look through them, and he said he was fine with that, so I'm heading over to his house in less than an hour. You can come if you want."

I'd slept in and had only consumed one cup of coffee so I knew I should decline but found myself agreeing to go. It would be interesting to look through the old newspapers and if it would help us identify our skeleton, even better. It was beginning to look as if the man in the walled-in room had been a lumber mill worker who'd lived and worked in the area right around the time the Westons and the Wades were striking it rich. If one of the local workers had turned up missing, maybe the man who put out the monthly paper would have reported about it.

If I was going to go with Tony, I needed to hurry up and get ready, so I poured a second cup of coffee and then ran upstairs to shower while Tony walked the dogs.

"So do you think that if this man went missing, his disappearance would have made the newspaper?" I asked as we drove toward Wade's mansion.

"Yes, I think something like a missing person would have made the newspaper."

"But why would this lumber mill worker even be at the Vandenberg house?"

Tony turned onto the country road that would take us out to the Wade property. "My theory is that this man, whom I am assuming at this point engaged in manual labor of some sort, came to the area to find work, and somewhere along the way, he met Ethel Vandenberg. I imagine that Ethel was lonely living in the big old house with only her abusive father for company, so when she met this young man, she struck up a friendship. Maybe they even fell in love. In one scenario, Edward was not at all happy with the fact that his upper-class daughter had found love with a common laborer, so he killed his daughter's suitor and hid the body."

I smiled. "That sounds like the plot for a historical romance."

"Fictional plots are based on someone's reality. It's a bit fantastic as far as theories go, but at the present time, it's the only one I have. I don't suppose you have a better one?"

"What if the man was a servant of the house? A groundskeeper or a stable hand as we discussed before. Maybe he witnessed Edward beating Ethel, so he tried to protect her and was killed for his effort."

"I suppose that works as well," Tony admitted. "Of course, I suppose we should keep in mind that the killer wasn't necessarily Edward. For all we know, he'd gone back to England by the time this man died, and the killer was Ethel."

"Okay, then maybe this stable hand tried to come onto her, and she stabbed him and then hid the body."

"Perhaps," Tony agreed. "Really, unless we are incredibly lucky and stumble onto something concrete, the reality is we'll probably never know the skeleton's identity or his story."

It made me sad that Tony was probably right. I guess all we could do at this point was to keep looking and hope that we stumbled onto something.

Wade was waiting for us when we arrived. He showed us into the library where someone had laid out the leather-bound books containing the newspapers. He offered us a beverage, instructed us to ring the bell should we need anything, and then left, promising to check back in with us in a bit. I'd been inside the Wade library on one other occasion and had to admit the place was impressive. There were floor to ceiling bookshelves with ladders that slid along each wall, a huge rock fireplace, dark wood tables and chairs, and a truly impressive desk.

"So where do we start?" I asked Tony after we were both seated.

"I guess we just start going through the books and if we see an article that seems to have promise, we'll pause and look at it together."

I settled in with the first book I'd selected, and Tony settled in with his. It really was pretty interesting to look at the articles that had been written all those years ago. There were a lot of mentions of the Weston and Wade families, but there were also mentions of other old-timers I'd heard about from the older folks in our community.

"Did you know that fourteen lumber mill workers died in a fire after they were cut off from the road while out surveying and marking the area for a future harvest?" Tony asked.

"No. I hadn't heard," I answered. "I suppose that there might have been a lot of tragedy back then. Harvesting trees is not easy work. If I had to guess, the odds of being hurt or killed while working in the field must have been pretty high. The equipment they had to fight a forest fire once it got started would be nothing like what we have nowadays, and there are still a lot of deaths due to uncontrolled fires."

Deciding to move on from this depressing subject, I returned my attention to the book I'd been looking through. I found I enjoyed the articles about births, marriages, community picnics, and barn dances a lot more enjoyable than the reports of deaths and other local tragedies. Of course, I guess that was true even today.

"Oh, look. Here is a photo of a new community church. I know it no longer stands, so it must not have stood the test of time, but I love the feel of the tiny building that was apparently erected in a single weekend by a group of volunteers." I continued to look at the photo. It looked like the entire town had come out. I focused in on the caption beneath the photo. "Apparently, Ethel Vandenberg donated the money to buy the materials to build the church."

Tony stopped what he was doing. "It lists her name specifically?"

"It does."

"That seems to indicate to me that Edward was already out of the picture whether he'd gone back to England, or died, or whatever. If he'd still been in the picture, then chances are he would have been named as the benefactor and not his daughter. When was the church built?"

"June of nineteen forty-eight."

"Okay. That helps us narrow things down. Does the article say anything else about Ethel?"

I continued to read. "No. Not really." I focused in on the photo. "Although, this woman in the center of the pack could be her. She is dressed nicer than everyone else, and the woman in the photo looks to be in her late thirty's. Ethel would have been thirty-seven when this photo was taken."

Tony got up and came around the table. He looked over my shoulder. I pointed to the photo.

"It does look as if this could be her," he said. "Who is that standing next to her?"

I searched for a name but didn't see one. "I have no idea, but it does appear as if they might be together. See how their shoulders are touching? And it sort of looks like he has an arm around her waist, but there are so many people crammed into one small area that it is hard to tell."

Tony frowned and walked back around the table to the book he'd been looking at. "Hang on. I think I know something." He flipped back a few pages and then carried the book around the table and set it next to mine. "Doesn't this guy," he pointed to a photo in his book, "look like he could be the same guy as this guy?" he pointed to the man standing next to Ethel in the photo in my book.

I looked at both photos. "It does look like the same guy."

"The newspaper I am looking through is from August of nineteen forty-eight. The photos are of the men who lost their lives in the fire. It appears as if Ethel's friend's name was Conway Crockett."

I glanced at Tony. "So this man who looks to be a friend of Ethel's is killed in the fire that killed fourteen men. That's so tragic." I paused to roll the idea around in my head. "Does it say how the fire started?"

Tony looked at the article. "Arson."

"So maybe Ethel figured out who started the fire and went after them. Maybe the body in the secret room was put there by Ethel as retaliation for killing this man who was her friend."

Tony looked doubtful. "I don't know. Even if Ethel did figure out who was responsible for the fire and desired to make him pay for what he'd done, how did she get him to the house? How did she get him up into the attic? And how did she overpower and stab him? And even if Ethel did kill this man, why entomb him in the house where she continued to live for more than a decade? Why not just bury him somewhere?"

"Yeah, I guess the idea is pretty out there. If you really think about it, it would have been pretty creepy for Ethel to have continued to live in the house knowing there was a dead body just upstairs."

Tony sighed. "We must be missing something that would explain why the body was in the sealed secret room which provided the only access to the clock tower other than the ledge which connected the clock tower and the widow's walk."

A thought occurred to me. "Do we know how long ago the clock stopped working?"

"I have no idea. Why?"

"Maybe the fact that the body was encased in a room which eliminated access to the clock tower and the fact that the clock stopped working are related. I know the clock hasn't worked for as long as I've been around."

"So you think the clock stopped working when the man died and was entombed in the room, and someone, probably Ethel, sealed up the secret room and the entrance to the clock tower in a room with no means of access?"

"It's a theory."

"Okay, so who is the guy, who killed him, how did his death stop the clock, and why did whoever sealed the guy in the room do so rather than just burying him?"

"I have no idea."

I got up and began to pace around the room. The idea that Ethel entombed the body really didn't work if you took into account the fact that she continued to live alone in the house for a lot of years after the body would have been left there. Even if she had killed someone and wanted to hide the body, there had to have been a better place to hide it. We suspected that Edward might have sealed off the narrow staircase that led to the widow's walk after his first wife fell or was pushed from it. If that were the case, the clock tower would have still been accessible from the ladder in the attic, assuming the secret room had actually been built in the forties and did not exist until quite a bit after the staircase was sealed. I'd been told that Ethel's mother, Barbara, fell down the stairs and died in nineteen eighteen, leaving Ethel in the house alone with her father. Of course, Ethel would only have been seven when her mother died. It really didn't make sense that a rich man such as Edward Vandenberg would raise his young daughter on his own. There must have been servants living in the house as well.

"I just had a crazy thought," I said.

"And what is that?" Tony asked.

"We know that Ethel's mother died in nineteen eighteen and we know that Edward continued to live in the house for some amount of time after that. We still don't know when he disappeared from the scene, and to tell you the truth, that is a piece of information I'd be interested in finding, although when he left or was killed or whatever is not the point I am trying to make. The point I am trying to make is that based on what we know of Edward, he does not appear to have been a celibate man, yet a third wife is never mentioned. What if Edward had a mistress? Maybe even more than one. What if his dalliances resulted in the birth of a child? A bastard child? What if Edward kept this child locked up in the house until he died when he was in his twenties?"

"Why would he do that?" Tony asked. "He was a single man after his wife passed, so there would have been no reason to hide a child conceived out of wedlock."

"I guess that's true. Unless the man in the room was Ethel's son."

Tony frowned. I could tell he was considering the idea. If Ethel had a son early in life, say during her teens, then conceivably she could have had a child in his late teens by the late nineteen-forties when we suspected the room had been constructed. "Do you think Ethel bore her father's son?"

"It's an unpleasant thought, but we've heard rumors that Edward abused Ethel. What if his abuse was not confined to beatings? What if, as a teen, Ethel became impregnated, and the result of that pregnancy, was a child that was forever hidden from the world?"

"Okay, say that very disturbing thought is true. If the son died as the result of a stab wound, who killed him? Edward?"

"Perhaps. Let's keep looking and see if we can narrow down the timeline a bit."

It took us another full hour to find the next clue, which came in the form of a small side note to an article about expansion at the lumber mill owned by Weston and Wade. The note related to the fact that Edward Vandenberg had actually been the one to first bring logging to the area, but that he'd shut down his mill in nineteen forty-two when he returned to England. If Edward was gone from the scene in nineteen forty-two, could he have killed the man in the attic before that? Assuming that Ethel would have had to have been at least thirteen when her baby was born, if that is even what happened, the baby would have had to have been born in nineteen twenty-four or later. If he'd been born in nineteen twenty-four, he would have been eighteen when the populace of what was to become White Eagle last saw evidence of Edward Vandenberg in the area. Tony called his guy in DC, who confirmed that in his opinion, the skeleton sealed in the secret room had been between sixteen and twenty-two when he died. The timeline fit. Of course, the fact that the timeline fit in no way constituted proof, and to be honest, I had no idea how we were ever going to get that.

"We need to speak to Bella Bradford," I said.

Bella Bradford was one of White Eagle's oldest residents and one of the only people who would have been both alive and old enough to remember what might have been going on at the Vandenberg house in the nineteen-forties.

Chapter 20

Bella Bradford lived in a cheery house that had wonderful curb appeal. I didn't know her exact age and wasn't inclined to ask, but my best guess was somewhere in her late eighties or early nineties. Either way, she would have most likely known Ethel in some capacity since Bella had lived in White Eagle her entire life.

"Sure, I remember Ethel. She was a very nice woman who lived a tough life but still managed to give back to the community. I don't know whether you've come across this in your investigation, but once Ethel's father left the area and Ethel was free to do what she chose, she donated a lot of money to help support projects in the community."

"I did read that she'd donated the money to build the church and some other structures which, unfortunately, were burnt down not all that long after."

Bella nodded. "It is true there was an arsonist in the area for a while. Such a tragedy."

"Do you remember when Ethel's father left White Eagle?" I asked.

Bella tapped her chin with her index finger. "Hmm. Let me think about this. I know the man lived in that big old house when Ethel was a child. He used to beat her, you know. Everyone in the area knew what was going on in that house, but no one took the initiative to stop him. I know that Ethel's mother died when she was seven or eight, and it seems as if Ethel's father stayed around until she was an adult." Bella paused, and her eyes narrowed. She took a sip of her tea as if allowing her mind time to work out the timeline. "I think Mr. Vandenberg had left the area by the time Ethel started openly dating Conway, which was just shortly before she donated the funds to build the church."

"The man who died in the fire?" I asked.

"Yes. You've heard of him?"

"We found an old newspaper article which listed the names of all the men who died in the fire. We recognized Conway from the photo of Ethel and a group standing in front of the newly constructed church before it burned down."

"Ethel and Conway were good friends even before they started dating. I'm not exactly sure when they met, but Conway's father worked for Mr. Vandenberg, and it seems to me that the two knew each other from the time they were children. Of course, Mr. Vandenberg would have nothing of Ethel dating anyone while he was around, so the poor woman was into her thirties before she was allowed to spread her wings and enjoy all that life had to offer."

"Do you know if Ethel had a younger brother? A much younger brother?" I decided not to bring up the possibility Tony and I had discussed about the body in the sealed secret room being Ethel's child unless the idea seemed warranted.

"There was talk of a child. As you've indicated, the rumor pertained to a child much younger than Ethel. I'm not sure how the child came to be in the house or even how old he was, but I do remember my friend, Evette, who worked for the Vandenberg family as a maid commenting that Mr. Vandenberg was keeping a young boy locked up in the attic."

I frowned. "He kept this child in the attic?"

Bella nodded. "The only people allowed into the attic were Ethel and her father. Evette seemed to think the child suffered from some sort of a developmental disorder. She never had the opportunity to meet the child, but she did say the sounds coming from the room were not the sounds that would be made by a normal child."

"Do you have any idea what happened to the child?" I asked.

"He seemed to disappear about the same time Mr. Vandenberg went back to England, so I imagine the child went with his father when he left."

Tony and I spoke to Bella a while longer, but she didn't seem to know anything that would conclusively prove that the body in the secret room was this child, or whether or not the boy in the attic was Ethel's son or her bastard brother. If the boy had been born with some sort of disorder that would not make him fit to be integrated into normal society, I could totally see someone as cruel as Edward Vandenberg locking him away out of sight. I could also imagine a situation where violent behavior was a symptom of the disorder, and as the child approached manhood, he became increasingly hard to control. In this scenario, it could have been either Edward or Ethel who killed the boy in self-defense.

During the ride home, we discussed the situation. "I really don't think there is a way to find out exactly what occurred all those years ago," I said. "I suppose we can assume that the body in the secret room is the body of this child who'd grown into a young man by the time he died. Perhaps Ethel's father killed the boy, and then left the area, or perhaps he killed the boy, and then Ethel killed her father and buried the body somewhere."

"Why would Ethel bury her father's body but entomb the body of the child that had been living in the house?" Tony asked.

"Maybe she cared about the child. Whether he was her son or her brother, she did live with him in that house with only the father for company. They may have been quite close even if the boy did suffer from some sort of developmental disorder."

"It is also possible that the father did return to England, leaving Ethel to care for this man child and she was the one to have ended up plunging a knife in his chest," Tony pointed out.

"I did think of that." I let out a slow breath. "I really do think this is one of those instances where we might never have our answers. Everyone who really knew what happened is dead, and it doesn't appear that Ethel left behind any sort of diary or journal."

"If she did, it is long gone. The house was emptied of any personal possessions left when the Jordans moved in."

"Which also means that if Ethel left a treasure as some in the area suspect, the Jordans most likely found it," I pointed out.

"True. Of course, the fact that the skeleton was still entombed in the secret room means that the Jordans never found the room or the secret passage, so if they didn't find the room or the passage, then it stands to reason they may not have found the treasure, if it even existed, either."

I supposed Tony had a point. "I guess we should go home and check on the animals and then get to the haunted house. I've really enjoyed the event, but I have to admit I will be happy when the event is over, and we can get back to our normal routine."

"This has been a labor-intensive fundraiser, but I think we've raised a lot of money."

"Oh, we have," I confirmed. "More than I ever thought possible; thanks to *Haunted America* and the free publicity they provided."

Chapter 21

Sunday, October 27

Tony and I both found it frustrating that we'd most likely never know the details relating to the skeleton in the secret room, but some mysteries really aren't meant to be solved and after discussing it in depth, we'd both decided this was one of them. It had occurred to us at some point along the way, that if Edward Vandenberg had taken his wealth and returned to England, then Ethel wouldn't have had all that cash to give away, so given the fact that the man just seemed to disappear, we both assumed he'd died, and Ethel had covered it up. The only reason we could think of for her to have covered it up was if she had killed her father, or perhaps someone she cared about, such as the boy in the attic, or perhaps her friend, Conway, had killed her father. If any of the three had killed the abusive man, I would assume his murder would have been justified, so I didn't feel a great need to prove this one way or another. Tony had done an extensive search for Edward Vandenberg after he'd supposedly left town, but was unable to find mention of him in any country. For all we knew, the man might very well have been buried somewhere on the Vandenberg property.

"Is Mike coming?" I asked Bree after she arrived alone for the haunted house that evening.

"He is going to meet us here. He had an idea relating to Joe Brown's murder that he wanted to check out, but he assured me he should be here by the time we start."

I glanced at my watch. It was five-thirty now. The event started at six, but if Mike had a lead on Joe's murder, that was definitely more important. "Any idea what he figured out?" I asked.

"He didn't say, but I did overhear him speaking to Frank on the phone, and they were discussing Joe's phone, or more specifically, his wife's phone. I'm not really sure why the fact that Joe had used his wife's phone to email Grange was important, but Mike seemed to think he was onto something."

I frowned. "I guess I can see where Mike is coming from. Joe wanted to go back to the house that evening to check something out, and he knew he'd need help, so he texted Grange who is the one who'd told him about the house and the treasure in the first place. His phone was not only dead, but he'd left it in his truck, so he used his wife's phone which she'd left sitting on the coffee table to text Grange. Grange, however, had been bowling and had not seen the text, but someone saw the text and answered on Grange's behalf saying they would meet Joe at the house. The person who answered Grange's phone deleted the text chain from Grange's phone so Grange never even knew he'd received the text. I have to assume that it was this person who then met Joe."

"Sounds right," Bree said.

"I wonder if Grange has a security code or fingerprint entry for his phone? If he does, it seems unlikely that anyone other than Grange could have sent the return text. If that is true, then Grange must have lied about not seeing the text, and the only reason to lie would be if he actually was the one to have killed Joe."

"Not everyone has security on their phone," Bree pointed out. "I didn't until I married Mike and he made me add it. I found the whole typing in a passcode thing to be too cumbersome, and it wasn't like there was anything important on my phone."

"Yeah, it is a pain to have to type in a passcode every time you just want to check your email, but phones are stolen and easily lost, so it does seem like a necessary precaution. Still, some people know my passcode. Tony for one and my mom since I asked her to check something for me when I left my phone at her house. Maybe someone had Grange's passcode."

"Like who?" Bree asked. "He isn't married."

"No, but he probably uses his phone for his business, and he does have a business partner."

Bree's eyes widened. "Greg."

I nodded. "I know Grange said he wasn't angry at Joe for leaving to start his own business, but I've also heard that Greg is furious. Tony found out that since Joe left, the company has been experiencing some financial hardship. Grange wasn't sure where he'd left his phone that night. He admitted that he often lost track of the dang thing. What if he left it on his desk? We know he was bowling when the text came through, but what if Greg was working late and saw the text on the lock screen when it came through. If he knew Grange's passcode, or if Grange doesn't use a passcode, he could have answered Joe pretending to be Grange and then met Joe at the house and killed him."

"Makes sense," Bree acknowledged. "I bet that is what Mike figured out as well." Bree's smile faded. "He really should have been here by now, or he should have at least called if he got held up. Do you think something's happened?"

Suddenly, at that moment, all I could think about was Mike being shot and left for dead the last time he'd gone after a killer. "I'm sure he is fine, but maybe we should call him and check in."

Bree nodded. She pulled out her phone and called Mike. The call went straight to voicemail. Then she called Frank, but his phone was off as well. "I'm worried," Bree said.

"Me too. Let's get Tony, and go and look for him. Brady can oversee things here."

Once I located Tony and informed Brady what we were doing, Tony, Bree, and I headed toward Greg Plimpton's house. The house was dark, and there were no cars in the drive, so we headed toward the office Greg and Grange used for their construction business, but it dark and empty.

"I think we should ask Grange if he knows where Greg might be," I suggested.

Tony looked up his number and made the call. He didn't answer, so we decided to go by his house just in case he'd left his phone somewhere, which is a behavior he'd already admitted he frequently engaged in. When we arrived at his home, we found his truck in the driveway, so the three of us approached the house.

"Hey, guys," he greeted after answering the door. "What can I do for you?"

"We're looking for Mike, whom we believe to be with Greg. We hoped you might know where he could be," I said.

"I'm not sure. I was finishing up some bids in the office earlier, and Greg was there with Olivia, but he didn't mention Mike."

"Who is Olivia?" I asked.

"Greg's ex. She works for the company as a bookkeeper."

"Seems awkward," Bree said.

"It can be, but Olivia has worked for Plimpton Construction longer than I have. She was originally hired by my dad, so she has worked for the company since before she and Greg were married. It didn't seem right to fire her when she and Greg divorced, so they've found a way to be civil to one another."

"I see." I glanced at Tony. He shrugged. "Do you know if Greg planned to go somewhere after he left work today?"

Grange frowned. "I'm not sure. Have you checked his home and the office?"

"We have," I answered.

"We do have a new speck house out past highway twelve. Greg and Olivia were discussing tile versus granite for the countertops. They might have gone out to take a look."

"Can you give us directions?" I asked.

"Sure. You just head out of town until the main highway crosses twelve. Take a left and go about a mile. There is a large two-story house under construction. A Plimpton Construction sign is in the front. You can't miss it."

"Okay, thanks," I said and then turned to leave. I turned back. "By the way, I know this is an odd question, but do you have a passcode on your phone?"

"Yeah. The way I leave the dang thing laying around, I need one. Why do you ask?"

I lifted a shoulder. "Just curious. Does anyone other than you have the code?"

"Greg and Olivia. My buddy, Cox, and this woman I used to date named Helen. Probably a few others. Why?"

"No reason. Thanks for taking the time to chat with us. Will you be at the haunted house for the finale on Thursday?"

"You know, I will."

After we left Grange's house, we headed toward the spec house. The closer we got, the tighter the knot in my stomach became.

"Based on the expression on your face, you're working on a new scenario or a twist to the old one," Tony said.

"Not really," I answered. "But I do have a new suspect in mind that hadn't occurred to me until this point."

"Olivia," Bree said. "When Grange mentioned her, it was like a light went on."

"Mike looked into the financials of Greg and Grange, as well as the company. We've established that the company is struggling, but Mike also mentioned that Greg was struggling personally due to his divorce. If Joe leaving hurt both the bottom line of the company and Greg's personal bottom line, it must have affected Oliva's income as well. I guess I assume she gets income from both the company she works for and her ex."

"Do you really think Joe was killed by Greg's ex?" Tony asked.

"It makes as much sense as anything," I answered. "And Joe most likely wouldn't have been leery about going up to the clock tower with Olivia, whereas, given the fact that Greg has been openly hostile toward him, I would think he might have proceeded with caution. But if Joe had worked for the company for a long time as Olivia had, the two might even have been friends."

"Or lovers," Bree piped in.

"Yes," I answered. "I suppose there could be that as well. An affair might even explain why Greg and Oliva broke up."

When we arrived at the spec house, we found Mike's car in the drive. If Greg was here, he must have parked his truck elsewhere. Tony suggested that Bree and I wait in his truck while he checked things out. Of course, neither of us did as he suggested and followed him down the drive and into the house. The front door had been left open, allowing access.

"Mike," I called.

We all paused to listen.

"Did you hear that banging?" Bree asked.

"It sounded like it was coming from downstairs," Tony answered. "There must be a basement." Tony took a step forward. "Stay behind me," he instructed.

I fell in directly behind Tony and Bree fell in behind me. When we arrived in the basement, it was dark. Tony found the switch and turned the lights on.

"Mike!" Bree screamed, running forward.

I followed behind. Mike was tied up and gagged, but he looked fine. Greg, on the other hand, was lying dead on the floor.

"What happened?" I asked after pulling off Mike's gag while Tony worked on the ropes that bound his hands and feet.

"Olivia happened. I had the idea that Greg might have killed Joe, so I called, and asked to speak to him, and he told me to meet him here. When I arrived, Greg was already dead. Olivia had a gun. She had Frank tie me up and then she left with Frank."

I frowned. "Frank was in on this?"

"No. Olivia took him out of here at gunpoint." As soon as Mike's feet were free, he stood up. "We need to find him. We need to find both of them."

"We will," I said.

Mike got on the radio and called Gage. He told him to put out an APB on Olivia, Frank, and the car Olivia was driving.

Chapter 22

Wednesday, October 30

"This is nice," Tony said as we snuggled on his sofa with the dogs and cats. It was a cold and rainy night, which was pretty perfect for our annual Halloween Spookathon.

"It is nice, and the fire is lovely, but I do hope the storm blows through before the haunted house tomorrow. I'm really hoping for a strong finale."

Tony passed me the popcorn. "According to the weather report, we should wake to sunny skies and mild temperatures."

"That's perfect," I said, popping a piece of the salty treat into my mouth. "I really have enjoyed doing the haunted house, but to tell you the truth, I'm going to be really happy to wrap it up as well."

"It will be nice to have our lives back," Tony agreed. "Of course, your mom is already hitting me up for help with Christmas on Main, so the break will be brief."

"I thought the committee hired someone to oversee the whole thing."

"They did," Tony answered, "but all the woman is really doing is organizing the volunteers. Apparently, it is up to the committee to recruit the volunteers. When I ran into her, she mentioned that she had signed both of us up for several different duties beginning with the setup, which includes enhancing the electrical and building the Santa house."

I guess I should have known that I wasn't going to be able to attend the event as a mere spectator. "I guess I don't mind helping as long as I don't have to dress up as an elf."

Tony grinned. "I think an elf costume would look cute on you."

"Never going to happen. Mike did take a few of the Santa shifts in the past, and I can see him doing it again. If he does, Bree can be his elf." I smiled. "I remember one year when the committee was desperate, and Frank ended up being the elf."

Tony chucked. "How is Frank doing anyway?"

"He's doing well. He had to have quite a few stitches in his head, and he suffered a few bumps and bruises when he rolled out of the vehicle Olivia was driving, but nothing that won't heal in a few weeks."

"I guess it's a good thing that family from Topeka saw him hit the pavement and got him to the hospital right away. It could have been so much worse."

My heart sped up just a bit. "Yes. It could have been a lot worse. He actually had lost a lot of blood from the head wound by the time they got him to the hospital."

"Any news about Oliva?" Tony asked as a commercial came on.

"I spoke to Mike when I delivered his mail this afternoon. He said she is still in a coma. I'm sorry she ran her car into a wall when she realized there was a police car chasing her, and I really do hope she pulls out of it and makes a full recovery, but even if she does wake up, all she is really waking up to is a very long time in prison. Not only did she confess to intercepting the text meant for Grange and killing Joe, but she killed Greg and kidnapped Frank as well. If he hadn't acted when he did, he might very well have died from the head wound she inflicted while trying to get him into her car, and then she would be looking at three murder charges, and one of those would have been a cop."

"Sometimes, I have to wonder what goes through people's heads to make them act the way they do. Joe was her friend. He had been her friend for a very long time. Why would she kill him?"

I shrugged. "I don't know. I suppose we might never know, just like we will most likely never know what happened to the young man who ended up entombed in the attic of the Vandenberg house."

Tony turned, so he was looking directly at me. "Actually, I do know what happened to the man in the attic. I was going to wait until later to tell you since we had a nice evening planned and the story is actually pretty ugly."

I just looked at Tony, confused as to where he was going with this.

"Remember two commercial breaks ago when I excused myself to return a call?"

"Yeah."

"It was a buddy of mine who collects handwritten contracts, letters, diaries, ledgers, or any other original document dating back to nineteen fifty or before. He is also part of an online group that collects similar items, and they have a chat room where they share information. I told him what I was after and he agreed to do a search to see if he could find anything leading back to either Edward or Ethel Vandenberg."

"Did he find something?" I asked.

Tony nodded. "He did. He actually found a man who owned a diary written by a woman named Cecilia Worthington. Cecilia lived in the area currently known as White Eagle from nineteen forty until nineteen fifty-two. She moved to Denver in nineteen fifty-two, and when she died in nineteen eighty-six, her daughter sold the fifty-two diaries she'd kept from nineteen thirty-four to nineteen eighty-six as part of the estate sale to liquidate her mother's assets."

I sat forward, giving Tony my full attention. "Did Cecilia know Ethel?"

Tony nodded. "She did. And based on what Cecilia knew, I suspect they were close. Cecilia's mother worked for Ethel as a cook between nineteen forty until somewhere around nineteen fifty. Based on what my friend was able to find out, Ethel and Cecilia became friends, and at some point for reasons unbeknownst to him, Ethel shared her deepest, darkest secret with Cecilia."

I couldn't help but hold my breath. "And?" I asked in a soft voice.

"Unfortunately, we were correct in our assumption that the skeleton in the secret room was Ethel's child. About a year before her mother died,

Edward began sexually abusing his daughter. When her mother found out, she tried to leave with Ethel, but as she tried to get away, Edward pushed his wife down the stairs and then told everyone she'd fallen. Ethel was too scared to say anything, so she didn't. Her father continued to sexually and physically abuse her until she became pregnant with his child when she was only thirteen. Her father sequestered her in the house and didn't allow her to see anyone, including the help while she was pregnant. She delivered her baby by herself while riding out a violent thunderstorm that occurred one night when her father was away. According to what Ethel told Cecilia, she believed the universe was angry about the birth of the child. Ethel told Cecilia that at the exact moment her baby was born, a bolt of lightning struck the house, damaging the clock which has never worked since."

"Oh, god. That poor thing."

"It gets worse," Tony warned me. "I guess the baby wasn't right. Ethel was sure the reason he wasn't right and the reason he was delivered into the world during a lightning storm, was because he was conceived in sin."

"What do you mean by not right?" I asked.

"Either Ethel didn't specify, or Cecilia didn't share the details in her journal, but it sounds as if the boy was both mentally and physically challenged. Edward didn't want anyone to know about the boy, so he kept him in the attic, and the only one who was allowed to visit with him was Ethel, who saw to his care."

I shook my head in disbelief. I really couldn't imagine.

"As the boy aged, he became physically stronger and much harder to control. Edward was afraid the boy was going to hurt someone, so he decided to kill him. By this point, the boy was able to physically stand up for himself, and a struggle ensued. According to Cecilia's account, Ethel tried to stop her father and shot him in the back as he stabbed his son. Edward left the house after Ethel threatened to finish him off, and based on what Ethel told Cecilia, she never saw him again. She assumed he was dead, but she wasn't certain. After her son died, she had her friend, Conway, seal off part of the room which served to eliminate access to the damaged clock, and to create a permanent tomb within the walls of the house for her son."

"It sounds as if she loved the boy."

Tony's eyes softened. "I'm sure she did."

I sat back and stared at the television screen. "You know, I was really frustrated that we hadn't been able to dig up the details relating to the skeleton in the closet, but now I wish we hadn't. Ethel's story is a lot more horrific than any of the cheesy stories being played out on the screen tonight."

"I know." Tony glanced at the television screen. "Do you want to turn it off?"

"No. Not yet. My mind is too disturbed to go to bed, but let's find something lighter to watch for a while. Maybe a silly comedy with no real plot."

Tony held up the remote. "You got it. Silly and meaningless coming right up."

Chapter 23

Friday, November 1

"You look adorable," Bree said after I arrived at the haunted house after-party dressed as a bat.

"You too. Cinderella?"

"Sleeping Beauty."

"Ah. Well, it's an awesome costume." I looked around Brady's home, which was packed wall to wall with the volunteers he'd wanted to thank. The haunted house had wrapped up late last night, so he'd decided to do this Halloween themed party tonight. "Where's Mike?"

"He's over at the bar talking to the guy dressed as a zombie."

I glanced in that direction. "Mike came as Batman?"

Bree nodded. "I wanted him to come as my prince, but he was having nothing to do with that.

When I suggested a knight in shining armor as an alternative, he decided to come as the dark knight."

"I guess it works. Batman is a justice fighter, and so is Mike."

Bree smiled as she looked at her husband. "He is at that. And those tights are the best." She looked back in my direction. "By the way, where is Tony?"

"He got a call just as we were parking, so I decided to come inside and let him have some privacy."

"Privacy? Who is he talking to?"

"One of his clients. I'm not sure which one, but it sounds as if one of the large companies he set up the software for has a glitch in their system. I'm hoping it won't require an out of town trip to fix it, but based on what I heard, it sounds like he may need to be there in person to do what needs to be done. I guess we'll see." I smiled at a friend who waved in my direction. "By the way, speaking of trips, I spoke to Mom about Thanksgiving, and she is fine with a trip to the lake. I even suggested Grizzly Lake since, as you pointed out, they have a new resort and each of us could have our own little cabin, and she agreed. She is going to ask a friend to come with us, so she won't have to bunk alone."

"That's great. Did she say which friend?"

I frowned. "Actually, she didn't. I think Aunt Ruthie is planning to go to her son's. Maybe someone she knows from one of her clubs. I think she has several single friends. Anyway, I guess we should call tomorrow and make sure we can reserve three cabins. Tony and I are fine with something small, but Mom will want a two-bedroom and a large kitchen."

"I'll call and see what we can get. I'm really looking forward to this. The resort even offers spa treatments. What I wouldn't give for a facial and massage."

"Tony said they have horseback riding and kayaking on the lake, as well as awesome hiking. I'm going to miss my fur babies, but I'm pretty excited as well."

Bree frowned. "I didn't even think about what we were going to do with Leonard. I guess they don't allow animals?"

"They don't, but Shaggy is going to stay at Tony's to take care of our crew, so you can just bring Leonard over there."

"Do you think Shaggy can be trusted? Leonard is Mike's baby."

"He can be trusted. Besides Mari will be staying at the house with Shaggy, and you know how great she is."

Bree smiled. "What is their deal anyway? Are they friends? Are they dating?"

"Shaggy says they are friends, but if I had to guess, they are friends with benefits. I don't suppose it matters. Mari is great, and she seems to have had a really positive influence on Shaggy since she's been back in town."

Bree looked toward the door. "It looks like Tony is off the phone. I'm going to grab a drink. Brady made black martinis that are to die for."

I waited where I was as Tony walked toward me. He really did look awesome in his Dracula costume. Bree might have a dark knight, but I had myself a dark prince.

"How'd it go?" I asked.

"It's fine. I need to log on and check a few things tomorrow, but I'm pretty sure I can fix what I need to remotely."

"That's good. I was hoping you wouldn't have to go out of town."

"Actually, I still might have to, but for a different client. I won't know until Monday, so let's just enjoy the weekend and worry about it then."

"Sounds good to me."

Tony nodded toward the entry where one of the men who'd volunteered as Frankenstein walked in with a woman dressed as a black fairy. "Isn't that Star?"

I looked in the direction Tony had indicated. "Yeah, that's her."

"Did you ever decide if you were going to talk to her about your father?"

"Actually, I've given it a ton of thought, and I think I'm going to leave it alone, at least for now. I stopped by her shop this past week pretending to be looking for a gift for my mom, and I asked her about the packet of information she'd received. She told me she'd put it in her safety deposit box. She hadn't even looked at it. She said that her past was in the past and digging around in it had brought nothing but heartache, so she was going to put a pin in the whole thing for now. She did hang onto the file rather than destroying it, so that does mean she could change her mind at some point, but I think, for now, she is content to leave the past in the past, and so am I."

"That's great. I really think that is for the best."

"I'm going to make an effort to establish a friendship with her. Partly because she might be my sister and I'd like to get to know her better, and partly so it will be easier to monitor the situation. If it looks like she is going to dig in again, we can figure out what to do at that point."

"That sounds like a good idea, but be careful. I can see a lot of potential for emotional upheaval by getting close to this woman."

"I know. I did think of that."

"Should we get a drink?" Tony asked.

I nodded. "Lets. It's been a really difficult couple of weeks, and I, for one, could use a night of relaxation. A few of Brady's black martinis should do the trick."

"You know," Tony said, kissing my neck, "there are other ways to relax."

I smiled. "Yeah? What did you have in mind?"

He whispered in my ear.

I smiled. "Now that my dark prince sounds exactly like the sort of thing I would enjoy."

Next from Kathi Daley Books

Preview:

Milton Standoff was a tall man, with a thin build, long arms and legs, small eyes, and a sharp nose. The first time I met him, I couldn't help but notice that the man looked a lot like a stork or maybe a crane. He moved with slow precision, which mimicked his speech and manor. He was an odd fellow, that was for certain, but in spite of his arrogant manner, dismissive attitude, and razor-sharp way of speaking, I really couldn't understand how he'd ended up dead in my parlor.

"State your name please," a police officer I didn't recognize instructed. My good friend, Police Chief Colt Wilder, worked out of the tiny satellite office that covered the small town of Holiday Bay, but he'd been out of town for a few days, so emergency calls received by his office were routed to the main switchboard in the much larger town southwest of us.

"Abagail Sullivan, but you can call me Abby."

"And you own this inn?"

I nodded. "Yes. I own the *Inn at Holiday Bay*, my inn manager, Georgia Carter, runs the place, and my new employee, Jeremy Slater, lives on the property with his niece, Annabelle. Jeremy helps Georgia with day-to-day operations. He is the one who discovered Mr. Standoff this morning, and he is the one who called it in. I'm sorry. What was your name again?"

"Officer James."

"Are you in town covering for Colt, I mean Police Chief Wilder?"

"I work out of the regional office, and happened to be in the area when the call came through, so I responded."

"I see." I smiled so as to appear appreciative, but I really wished Colt were here. The inn had only been receiving guests for three months, so this was our first dead body. Actually, I hoped it would turn out to be our only dead body. "So what exactly do you need from me?"

"I need you to walk me through exactly what happened this morning," the man continued.

I nodded, took a deep breath, and began to speak. "Jeremy opened up the inn like he does every morning. He lives in the basement with Annabelle, so it is easiest for him to unlock the exterior doors, start fires in the three wood-burning fireplaces located on the first floor, and open the blinds and drapes before he has to leave to take Annabelle to school. As he does every morning, he was performing these chores when he noticed Mr. Standoff here laying on the floor in the parlor. He went in to investigate and found the man dead. It appears as if he's been hit over the head with the pilgrim that we had on display on the fireplace mantel."

The man jotted down a few notes while I tried to rein in my sudden need to ramble. Just answer the man's questions, I reminded myself, as I suppressed the urge to go off on a tangent about how I had bought the mansion sight unseen after my husband and son died in an automobile accident and how I'd not only found a new start but a new family here in Holiday Bay.

"And what time were the exterior doors locked the previous evening?" Officer James asked.

"Ten o'clock. Jeremy always does his walkthrough at ten o'clock. He noted in the logbook we keep that it appeared that all our guests were in for the evening when he locked the exterior doors, banked the fires, and dimmed the lights. When he began opening things up this morning, the exterior doors were still locked, and it didn't look as if anyone had accessed them since the previous day, although I suppose it is possible that Mr. Standoff hadn't been in his room during the walkthrough as Jeremy thought."

"I assume the guests have access to an exterior door even after hours?"

I nodded. "The back door leading into the kitchen can be opened with the room keys."

"Who else, other than you and your guests, has a key to the inn?" Officer James asked.

"Georgia, of course, and Jeremy. We have a part-time employee who helps with the cleaning. Her name is Nikki. She lives next door and is one of the sweetest people you will ever meet. She would not have killed this man."

"Anyone else?"

"I guess Lonnie has a key."

"Lonnie?"

"Lonnie Parker is my contractor. He oversaw the renovation of this place, and even though that part of the project is complete, he still pops in from time to time to take care of any repairs that might be needed. I can absolutely assure you that Lonnie wouldn't kill anyone."

The man paused, tapping his pen on his notebook. "Someone did."

"Well, yes, someone did, but I don't see why any of our guests would have done such a thing. Yes, Mr.

Standoff was an arrogant sort who'd managed to get on everyone's nerves, but to kill the man? I just don't see it happening."

Officer James continued to tap his pen against the small pad he held. He had a slow way about him that I found to be very annoying. Finally, he spoke. "I understand your need to protect your guests and employees, nevertheless, as I've already mentioned, someone killed this man. I'm going to need information on every employee and each of your guests, beginning with each person's full name and their reason for being in town."

"Okay." I took a breath and told him what I could about Georgia, Jeremy, and Nikki.

"And your guests?" He prompted.

"Let's see. A man named Gaylord Godfry is staying in unit six, which is the unit on the top floor in the area which previously served as the attic. He has been with us for more than two months. He is a retired history professor who is in the area to work on his novel."

The man jotted down a few notes. "Did it seem as if Mr. Godfry had a conflict of any sort with Mr. Standoff?"

"No. Not really. Well yes, I guess in a way he did."

The man looked at me over the top of his pad.

I elaborated. "As I already mentioned, Mr. Standoff was an arrogant and generally unlikeable sort. I guess his family has been around since the Mayflower, and apparently, he seemed to think that his lineage provided him with a unique knowledge of all things colonial. He would get into arguments with Gaylord over who settled where, when they settled, and how this particular pattern may have contributed to certain developments in United States history." I took a breath and then continued. "Gaylord has a doctorate in history. He taught the subject at a university level for years; whereas Mr. Standoff was nothing more than a washed-up actor in town to direct the annual Thanksgiving pageant. Of course, Gaylord knew more about the actual history of the area and of the United States as a whole than Standoff ever would, but the visiting director was just too arrogant to see it, so the men did spar from time to time."

"Spar?"

"Verbally. Not physically."

"In your mind, is it possible that the men may have both come downstairs for something to read or perhaps something to drink, and while they were both downstairs, an argument ensued, and Mr. Standoff ended up dead?"

"No," I answered without hesitation. "Gaylord would never kill one of our guests or anyone for that matter just because they were a self-entitled boob." I tapped down my irritation with this line of reasoning and tried to remind myself that the man was just doing his job. He didn't know Gaylord the way I'd come to know him, so he couldn't know that the man was perfectly harmless.

"Okay," Officer James continued. "Go on. Who else was staying in the inn last night?"

"As I already mentioned, Gaylord is staying in unit six. Our victim, Milton Standoff, was in unit five. Unit four is currently empty since the guests who were in that unit checked out yesterday, and no one is due to check in until the weekend. A man named Noah Daniels is in unit three. He is in town to interview for the head pastor position at the church. He is a very nice man, mid-thirties, and he has a calming and serene way about him. I don't know him well, but I would be willing to bet there is no way he would kill anyone."

Officer James continued to jot down notes. "Continue. What about units one and two?"

"Christy and Haley Baldwin are in unit two. Christy is in town so that her daughter can visit her grandparents. Christy's husband, Ron, died just about a year ago and his parents asked Christy to bring Haley to town so they could spend time with their granddaughter."

"And unit one?"

"Empty as well. We have a couple checking in on Thursday."

"So, in your opinion, none of the current guests would have been likely to have killed Mr. Standoff?"

I slowly shook my head. "No. As I've already stated, I really can't see that any of them would have done such a thing." I glanced at the sheet-covered human form laying on the floor. "I can't explain how anyone who was not a guest or employee could have gotten in here to kill this man, but I just don't think the killer was anyone we've spoken about."

"How long has Mr. Standoff been staying with you?"

"Almost two weeks. Like I said, he is in town to direct the pageant."

"And this pageant, is it an annual event?"

I nodded. If this man didn't know about the Holiday Bay Thanksgiving Pageant, he must be new to the area since our pageant was a well-known event throughout Northern New England. "The pageant is part of the week-long 'kick-off to the holidays' celebration' the town sponsors to lure tourists into the area. From what I understand, the town hosts the pageant every year on the weekend before Thanksgiving, but this is the first year they've brought in outside talent. Normally, Emma Johnson from the high school directs the play."

The officer looked at me. "Do you know why the town is doing things differently this year?"

I slowly shook my head. "Actually no, I'm not sure why the committee decided to bring Mr. Standoff in. I suppose he does provide a degree of name recognition. He was just in that movie with Denzel Washington. I can't remember the title. It was some sort of a thriller that I never did get around to seeing. And I think he did a movie with Will Smith a while back. Both movies were popular, but Standoff just had bit parts. Still, I suppose he has had bit parts in other movies as well. I think he might have been one of the villains in a Marvel movie. I imagine the committee figured that if they brought in a professional actor to direct the pageant, they might attract more spectators from the larger cities west of us."

"So, in the almost two weeks the man has been staying with you, have you been made aware of anyone who specifically might hold a grudge against him?"

"If you are looking for a list of individuals who will breathe a sigh of relief when they find out this man is no longer in the picture, you are going to need a bigger notebook. But wanting the man gone does not mean that the men and women who pour their hearts and souls into the pageant each year necessarily wanted him dead."

Officer James jotted down a few more notes. He paused and looked around the room. The pilgrim statue was still lying on the floor. He bent over and picked it up with a gloved hand. "It's heavy."

I nodded. "It's made of lead." I nodded toward the mantel where the female pilgrim still stood. "It's part of a set. Antiques. I've been told they are over a hundred years old."

I watched as the gloved officer slid the statue into an evidence bag.

"The fact that this man was hit over the head with an object close at hand indicates a crime of passion," Officer James stated. "If I had to guess, Mr. Standoff either ran into an employee or another guest after he'd come into the parlor for some reason. He argued with whomever he ran into, the employee or guest became angry, grabbed the pilgrim statue, and hit the man over the head with it."

I wrinkled my nose. "I really don't think it was a guest or employee that killed this man."

Officer James began tapping his pencil on his pad once again. It seemed to be a nervous habit. "Okay, if not a guest or employee, then who? According to what you just told me, no one else, except for your contractor, has a key to the place, and we've established that the murder occurred after Mr. Slater locked up for the evening."

"I suppose Mr. Standoff might have asked someone to meet him here. As I've already indicated, the doors are locked at ten p.m., but the guests have access to move about at will. All the exterior doors open from the inside, which would allow any guest to invite someone in, and, as I've already indicated, the keys to each suite open the back door which leads from the drive into the kitchen. We've set things up this way so that anyone who might still be out after we lock up, can get in. So as you see, it is totally possible Mr. Standoff invited someone to meet him here. If that is true, then the killer could really have been anyone."

Books by Kathi Daley
Come for the murder, stay for the romance

Zoe Donovan Cozy Mystery:
Halloween Hijinks
The Trouble With Turkeys
Christmas Crazy
Cupid's Curse
Big Bunny Bump-off
Beach Blanket Barbie
Maui Madness
Derby Divas
Haunted Hamlet
Turkeys, Tuxes, and Tabbies
Christmas Cozy
Alaskan Alliance
Matrimony Meltdown
Soul Surrender
Heavenly Honeymoon
Hopscotch Homicide
Ghostly Graveyard
Santa Sleuth
Shamrock Shenanigans
Kitten Kaboodle
Costume Catastrophe
Candy Cane Caper
Holiday Hangover
Easter Escapade
Camp Carter
Trick or Treason
Reindeer Roundup
Hippity Hoppity Homicide

Firework Fiasco
Henderson House
Holiday Hostage
Lunacy Lake
Celtic Christmas – *December 2019*

Zimmerman Academy The New Normal
Zimmerman Academy New Beginnings
Ashton Falls Cozy Cookbook

Tj Jensen Paradise Lake Mystery:
Pumpkins in Paradise
Snowmen in Paradise
Bikinis in Paradise
Christmas in Paradise
Puppies in Paradise
Halloween in Paradise
Treasure in Paradise
Fireworks in Paradise
Beaches in Paradise
Thanksgiving in Paradise – *October 2019*

Rescue Alaska Mystery:
Finding Justice
Finding Answers
Finding Courage
Finding Christmas
Finding Shelter – *Early 2020*

Whales and Tails Cozy Mystery:

Romeow and Juliet
The Mad Catter
Grimm's Furry Tail
Much Ado About Felines
Legend of Tabby Hollow
Cat of Christmas Past
A Tale of Two Tabbies
The Great Catsby
Count Catula
The Cat of Christmas Present
A Winter's Tail
The Taming of the Tabby
Frankencat
The Cat of Christmas Future
Farewell to Felines
A Whisker in Time
The Catsgiving Feast
A Whale of a Tail
The Catnap Before Christmas – *October 2019*

Writers' Retreat Mystery:

First Case
Second Look
Third Strike
Fourth Victim
Fifth Night
Sixth Cabin
Seventh Chapter
Eighth Witness
Ninth Grave

A Tess and Tilly Mystery:

The Christmas Letter
The Valentine Mystery
The Mother's Day Mishap
The Halloween House
The Thanksgiving Trip
The Saint Paddy's Promise
The Halloween Haunting
The Christmas Clause – *November 2019*

The Inn at Holiday Bay:

Boxes in the Basement
Letters in the Library
Message in the Mantel
Answers in the Attic
Haunting in the Hallway
Pilgrim in the Parlor – *October 2019*
Note in the Nutcracker – *December 2019*

A Cat in the Attic Mystery:

The Curse of Hollister House
The Mystery before Christmas – *November 2019*

The Hathaway Sisters:

Harper
Harlow
Hayden – *Early 2020*

Haunting by the Sea:

Homecoming by the Sea
Secrets by the Sea
Missing by the Sea
Betrayal by the Sea
Thanksgiving by the Sea – *October 2019*

Sand and Sea Hawaiian Mystery:

Murder at Dolphin Bay
Murder at Sunrise Beach
Murder at the Witching Hour
Murder at Christmas
Murder at Turtle Cove
Murder at Water's Edge
Murder at Midnight
Murder at Pope Investigations

Seacliff High Mystery:

The Secret
The Curse
The Relic
The Conspiracy
The Grudge
The Shadow
The Haunting

Road to Christmas Romance:

Road to Christmas Past

USA Today best-selling author Kathi Daley lives in beautiful Lake Tahoe with her husband Ken. When she isn't writing, she likes spending time hiking the miles of desolate trails surrounding her home. She has authored more than a hundred books in twelve series. Find out more about her books at www.kathidaley.com

Stay up-to-date:
Newsletter, *The Daley Weekly* http://eepurl.com/NRPDf
Webpage – www.kathidaley.com
Facebook at Kathi Daley Books –
www.facebook.com/kathidaleybooks
Kathi Daley Books Group Page –
https://www.facebook.com/groups/569578823146850/
E-mail – kathidaley@kathidaley.com
Twitter at Kathi Daley@kathidaley –
https://twitter.com/kathidaley
Amazon Author Page –
https://www.amazon.com/author/kathidaley
BookBub – https://www.bookbub.com/authors/kathi-daley

Printed in Great Britain
by Amazon